MW01596833

THE SHACK

THE SHACK

Thomas Mulholland

iUniverse, Inc.
New York Lincoln Shanghai

The Shack

Copyright © 2005 by Thomas Mulholland

iUniverse books may be ordered through booksellers or by contacting:

iUniverse
2021 Pine Lake Road, Suite 100
Lincoln, NE 68512
www.iuniverse.com
1-800-Authors (1-800-288-4677)

Author's Note:
Though the events depicted in this book bear some similarity to certain segments of my life, the characters and happenings are creations of my imagination. Any resemblance to real people or events is coincidental, and such resemblance is the product of the creative process.

ISBN-13: 978-0-595-35022-3 (pbk)
ISBN-13: 978-0-595-79727-1 (ebk)
ISBN-10: 0-595-35022-4 (pbk)
ISBN-10: 0-595-79727-X (ebk)

Printed in the United States of America

For Jennifer, Catherine, and Sarah

"Happiness and freedom begin with a clear understanding of one principle: some things are within our control and some things are not. It is only after you have faced up to this fundamental rule and learned to distinguish between what you can and cannot control that inner tranquility and outer effectiveness become possible...

...Remember too, that if you think you have free rein over things that are naturally beyond your control, or if you attempt to adopt the affairs of others as your own, your pursuits will be thwarted and you will become a frustrated, anxious and fault-finding person."

—Epicetus, Stoic Philosopher (In approx. 95 AD)

Prologue

You can't pick a flower without the trembling of a star.

—Unknown

Tonight the moon appears unusually bright and extraordinarily close. So close that I can in fact make out small details. Despite the brightness of the moon, the sky is bursting with stars. I like looking at the stars. I squint to see one tiny pinpoint of light. I wonder how far away it is. And the shooting stars, I've never seen so many. They're so vivid, streaking across the sky. I turn back to the fire where just a few minutes earlier I shared a few beers with friends. Well, the truth is I gave up beer a long time ago. Now I drink wine, just red wine—expensive red wine.

My friends Ralphie, Mitch, and Jake still drink beer, Blatz beer. I didn't know they still made the stuff. The guys kid me about drinking wine. "You one of those wine snobs now?" they ask.

I nod and chuckle. "Oh yeah, I'm a wine snob all right; only the best for me; nothing but the best."

I turn to Jake. I'm a little puzzled by his presence. I don't think he's supposed to be here. "Jake, I thought you were supposed to be dead, a car accident or something, right?" He just grins that big grin of his and lights another cigarette. The guy is all lips and teeth. I look at my friends and wonder how they have all stayed so young; they still look like teenagers. Mitch over there with that tuft of hair he calls his bangs.

"Mitch, when are you going to cut that thing hanging on your forehead?" He takes another swig of beer.

"I tell you what: I'll cut my hair when you decide to stop acting like an asshole." We laugh. But now my buddies are gone. I'm not sure where they've gone.

- 1 -

I look around. They're probably in the woods taking a piss, I think. Anyway, I'm saddened that they've decided to leave.

"Ah, screw 'em," I say. I can get on with some serious drinking now. I do most of my drinking alone anyway. I check the cooler just to be sure I have enough to drink. Yeah, there is plenty of wine, but what am I supposed to do with all this Blatz beer? I look out over the lake and notice a figure on the raft waving at me. *Jesus,* the water looks smooth and shiny, like black ice; son of a gun, I'll bet I could walk right over to the raft. I look up at the sky again; I wonder if the figure on the raft notices all the shooting stars. I smile to myself. I even feel a little giddy, like a little kid. I holler at the figure, "Hey, can you see the stars? Look at the stars!" I don't get any answer. I look towards the raft and squint, like I'm trying to make out a distant star, but I just can't make out who it is.

Jake is back, and he takes a drag from his cigarette. "We're going to The Shack for a while. You coming?"

"No. I don't think so," I say looking toward the raft.

Jake takes another drag. "Tommy, are you going out there?" he asks, pointing toward the water.

"Huh? Oh. Yeah, why not?" I say.

"Fuckin-A, man; you just know you're going to kill yourself."

No, I think I'd better check this out. I *need* to find out who is on the raft. I strip down to my underwear and start to walk into the water. I turn around, and they're all back, standing on the shore. "Tommy. Take it easy man."

As I look back at them I wonder if I'll see them again, and I'm overcome with a sense of sadness. "Thanks guys. See ya."

I turn and then someone says, "Tommy, you forgot your drink."

"You drink it," I say.

"I don't drink this shit," says Ralphie with a scowl. We laugh.

The water is warm, and it feels like silk on my body. This feels so good, I think to myself, I don't want it to end. I want to wrap my arms around it. Now I'm on the raft, and we've drifted farther out into the lake. Suddenly someone speaks from behind me. "We're too far out, and we can't get back," my mother says to me.

"Mom, what are you doing out here?" I ask. "You don't swim. How did you?..." Something's wrong with her; she doesn't look right. It occurs to me that she died a few years ago from cancer; it was a slow, agonizing death. What the hell? She looks ill, and she looks...sad. She's looking at me in a way that says, "I'm sorry." Sorry for what, I wonder.

She's wearing her glasses and that same old, tattered robe she has worn for years. I notice there are spots of blood on it. I wonder where the blood came from. This whole thing is odd. I wonder why she would swim out in her robe. Why is she wearing that thing anyway? "When are you going to throw that away?" I ask.

She doesn't answer my question, but instead she points to the water, "There's something out there you need to see."

What is she talking about? "Something out there I need to see?" I don't think I really want to see what's out there.

"I know you don't believe me. Go look for yourself," she insists. I look over the edge of the raft, and it's pitch black, and I can't see a damned thing. It's as if all the lights were just switched off. Then suddenly I'm falling through the darkness.

I catch a glimpse of something. The lights are switched back on. The moon is shining through water, and I just stare at it. The water is warm, and it feels good. It has shades of yellow and green. I feel secure here, and I don't think I want to leave. That moonlight, man, I don't think I've ever seen anything quite like it. I'm mesmerized by it, and I reach out to touch it. But it's just beyond my fingertips. I don't bother to swim; I just continue to watch myself fall through the water. Death isn't so bad, I think. God, that light is bright. And then I open my eyes, and the sun is shining through the bedroom window.

Michigan, 1968

My grief lies all within,
and these external manners of lament
are merely shadows to the unseen grief
that swells within

—William Shakespeare: *Richard II,* Scene 4

CHAPTER 1

My head is throbbing again. It hurts so much that I'm starting to get sick to my stomach. I get these headaches all the time, and aspirin never helps. My parents are fighting again, and I play the part of peacemaker. I'm sick and tired of playing this role, but I desperately try to make peace. I plead with them, "C'mon, you guys. Please don't fight." But I'm ignored.

There never was really a chance that they would stop. They've got tunnel vision, and they can't see beyond the next insult. "Why are you talking to Mom like that? You wouldn't talk like that to your friends." I ask at the risk of great bodily harm to myself.

"You just stay the hell out of this!" he says. I pace back and forth. "Kids, get in here." We congregate in, of all places, the family room. The irony is lost on them. "Your mother and I are getting a divorce, and you need to choose who you are going to live with."

Oh, God, not again! How many times do we have to do this? My stomach is in knots, my head is pounding, my breathing becomes difficult, and I'm sweating bullets. "You have to make a choice; who do you want to live with, your mom or your dad?"

"I don't. I can't." My younger brothers choose my dad for the same reason I will. My dad intimidates us.

It's winter, and my dad, my brothers, and I are playing hockey on the frozen lake. My dad lets us shoot pucks at him without any padding. He has a six pack of beer nearby; I suppose that helps. We're having a good time, or so I think. As we're playing, I knock my brother over. He doesn't take much offense. His fall really wasn't that hard anyway, but my dad does take offense. He walks over and, without warning, he knocks me down with a punch to the head.

The edges of the ice rink have small piles of half-frozen slush and shards of sharp ice here and there. I'm now on my knees thinking that this bastard is losing it again. "Let's see how you like it," he says as he takes the back of my head and drives my face into the slush and ice and mashes it around a bit. He finally lets up, and I'm left with cuts on my nose and lip. I smell the beer on his breath. There's blood running down my face, and I can taste it in my mouth.

For a split second I consider taking my hockey stick and hitting him in the head with it. I don't though. I just skate away. He hollers after me. "Where you going, mama's boy?"

"I'm getting the hell away from you."

So, I squirm, and I beg them not to do this. "Don't make me choose," I plead. I want to scream, pull my hair out, break windows, and take a baseball bat to both of them. I can see the hurt in my mom's face as my brothers make their choice. Will her wounds ever heal? The emotional wounds she has must run deep.

I excuse myself and run to the bathroom, where I vomit. I begin to sob, "*Why? Why?*" I don't understand what's going on here. I was having a good day and then. "*Goddamn it, this can't be happening again!*"

I return, and I'm asked to make a decision. They don't get it, do they? I seem to be getting tunnel vision. I'm exhausted, "Okay. Dad, I guess." My dad is in his glory; he has won, and my mom has lost this battle. What they are incapable of understanding is that no one wins in these matters. There are only losers.

Dear Tom,

Do remember the secret room? That was the place you could go and be safe. You walked upstairs toward your bedroom. At the top of the stairs was a closet. It was a deep closet where winter coats and the like were stored in the summer. You found an opening way back in the corner. You got through the opening, and there was the secret room. You went there sometimes when you had headaches. Those were bad headaches. No one could find you back there. You have pleasant memories of the room; sometimes you even dream of it. There was light in the room by which you read books, sometimes for hours. You read a book by John Kennedy, Profiles in Courage, and another about being an astronaut.

It was safe, and that was what was most important to you. Security, or the lack thereof, has followed you around all your life. Sounds like fear to me. I wonder what impact it's had on your life. What do you think? Tell me, what are your greatest fears?

Well, you did what you had to in order to survive. That was the primary objective then. No need to analyze it to death. You'll find the answers in due time.

Take care.

West Michigan, 1994

> *I always keep a supply of stimulant handy in case I see a snake—which I also keep handy.*

—W. C. Fields (1880–1946)

CHAPTER 2

What is it about water that is so hypnotic? I can sit next to it for hours. A lake, an ocean, a river, or a brook—it doesn't matter. I like the way it sounds, I like the way it looks, and I like the way the sun dances on it. The sun beats down on the back of my neck, helping the muscles in my shoulders and neck relax. Time passes quickly out here. I've been here for hours, but it seems like just a few minutes. I seem to be a long way from my troubles when I'm here. I've got the sounds of the water; the sun, and a warm breeze at my face. Troubles? What troubles? I look at my watch, and it's getting close to 5:00 PM. I should probably start home, but there's really no rush, is there?

In fact, there is. I get a little anxious around this time of day. My internal alarm has gone off. Despite the beauty all around me, this obsession I'm unable to manage is telling me that it is indeed time to leave.

The apartment is on the second floor of a hillside home. It's small with just three rooms, but it overlooks the big lake. The rent is unbelievably cheap, it's quiet, and I feel secure there. That, I suppose, is what I like the best about it. How much room does a single person need anyway? Besides, this is all about location. I get a kick out of telling people I live on the beach, "Oh, wow! You're kidding!"

"No, really," I say, "right on the beach." It makes me feel important somehow. I tell them that, on some nights, I open the windows, and the sounds of the lake help to put me to sleep. Sometimes I have difficulty going to sleep. Sometimes I'm afraid to go to sleep.

I'm driving down the road when I notice a figure standing on the sidewalk. I slow down to look. It's some man. I don't know who it is, I don't recognize the face, but this man is very sad. I can tell this man is in deep despair about something. I wonder what it is. Suddenly he draws a pistol and brings it to his head. What the hell? I'm overcome with fear and dread. Oh God, no, no! I cover my ears and look away. I don't want to hear this! Then, there's a loud crack. "Holy Jesus," I think. Blood splatters all over the windshield of the car. I bolt up in my bed; I'm breathing hard and sweating. Thank God, it was just a dream, just another dream.

On my way home from work, I make my usual stop at the liquor store, and I pick up a nice bottle of red wine. I look over the bottles as if I were some sort of connoisseur of the stuff, but I wouldn't know a good wine from a bad one. I don't think I have enough at home, so just to be sure…Yeah; much better to be safe than sorry. Once I get home and settled in, it's a pain in the ass to go out again. It's always better to have too much than too little. I had better pick something up. It seems to go this way everyday.

Well, maybe that's a poor choice of words and not totally accurate. Actually, that *is* the way it goes everyday. I change the liquor stores I go to now and then, but they recognize me when I walk in the door. "Mr. Carter, how are you today?" I lie.

"Real good. Thanks. How about you?" What am I supposed to say? "Life sucks, thanks for asking?" I fake a grin. "Oh, not too bad."

"We just got a new red wine you might want to look at."

"Terrific; I'll have a look," I say. "Good Christ, I wish he would just mind his own damn business," I think to myself. I'd prefer it if he would not talk to me at all. I try my best to avoid eye contact, but some people just can't take a hint.

I feel guilty and a bit ashamed about coming here so often. Guilt and shame give me two more reasons to have a drink. Not that I need another reason; any reason will do. It's Tuesday; that's reason enough. Sometimes I feel like maybe, just maybe, I have a drinking problem. Upon further reflection I decide I don't, though. Red wine, after all, is good for you isn't it? They said so on the news. How bad can fermented grapes be anyway?

"Man, I gotta find something else to drink; I can't keep drinking beer, the stuff goes right to my stomach," I say. I've noticed that I'm beginning to get a bit bloated. It's not just my stomach that's bloated, though. "I've started drinking wine," John, a friend of mine, says.

"Really? Why is that?"

"Tommy, wine is made from what?" He answers his own question, "Grapes, right?"

Right. Grapes. The guy was a genius. "How bad can it be for you?" he asks. "Can't be bad at all; not at all."

Although sometimes after waking up with a hangover, I think that perhaps it *is* no good for me. I've had it; no more.

Once in a while I visit a female friend who lives a short distance away. We have alcohol and sex in common, and that's good enough for me. Sometimes after dinner and a few drinks she talks about dancing on the beach in the middle of the night. "Dance on the beach? Why would you want to dance on the beach?"

"My dear Thomas," she says, holding my face in her hands, "because I can. Haven't you ever wanted to do something silly?" Me, do something silly? I figure she's got a screw loose. I do enjoy her company, but I have to deal with the guilt the next morning. I think guilt is the proper response here. I *should* feel guilty. I'm sure God is writing all of this down, and when my time comes I'm going to be called on the carpet.

"So Tom, it says here in my notes that you drank to excess and on occasion had sex with several different women. Did I get that right?" asks God.

"Well, I guess. But you see, it wasn't my fault," I answer.

"Uh-huh. What kind of relationship did you want from these women? Were you honest about your intentions?"

I stammer, "Okay; okay; no. I wanted sex. Jeez, is that so bad?"

"No," says God. "That's not so bad. I just wish you had been honest about it."

So the next morning I pop a couple of aspirin and a vitamin B_{12} with my coffee, and then I pour any leftover bottles down the sink. I feel good about that. It's time for a new start. There. I did it. All down the drain—again. A huge weight has been lifted from my shoulders. Shoot, I even feel a boost of energy. The sun is out; the sky is blue; it's a great day! But time heals all hangovers, and guilt is way overrated. By evening I'm feeling better, and I can handle another bottle or two.

Drinking problem? What drinking problem? I might even give my friend a call; maybe go to the local bar on the beach and have a few drinks watching the sun set, and commiserate about work. Screw it! I'm in terrific shape, and I cycle nearly every day. It's not as if I were sleeping in the gutter. I make it to work without any difficulty. Drinking problem? I don't think so.

I'm sick and tired of this circular self-talk; "you have a drinking problem," then "no, you don't have a drinking problem." I made it through graduate school, for crying out loud! Get over it! Once and for all. *I don't have a drinking problem.* I've quit for a week or perhaps even a month at a time. I have it under control. About those two trips to rehab—c'mon, I did that so that people would get off my back.

I open my eyes and find myself a bit disoriented. My mouth feels like sand, and my head is pounding. I recognize the long red hair of the woman I'm in bed with, but I don't know how I got here. "Good morning," she says, waking up.

"Oh. Yeah, good morning," I answer. I find my way to the bathroom where I vomit into the toilet. I look in the mirror and I'm disgusted with what I see.

"You okay in there?" she asks.

"Yeah, I'm okay." I puke again.

"I'm making breakfast. Do you want some eggs?" Can't she stop talking?

"No thanks." I come out of the bathroom and get dressed. "Leaving so soon?"

"Yeah," I say, "I gotta get going." I drive the fifteen miles home, run up the stairs, and fumble with the keys. I feel like I might vomit again. "Goddamned keys," I mutter to myself. Finally I get the door open, rush inside, and open the kitchen cabinet. I panic. I can't find the wine. Where's the wine? I open the refrigerator, and there it is. How in the hell did it get in the refrigerator? I don't keep wine in the refrigerator. I pour a glass and drink it straight down. I pour another and settle into a chair. I begin to feel a bit more human. I start to wonder if maybe I should be in rehab.

So after my trip to the liquor store, I make it home from work, and I change out of my suit and tie. I really hate wearing the corporate monkey suit, but it does make me look...important. Perception is reality isn't it? I pass people in my car on the way to work, and I imagine what they might be thinking. "There goes a very successful guy." What people think about me is important. Anyway I get a little exercise, take a shower, and turn on the television. For some reason I like it as background noise. I think of work and of an exchange I had with a coworker.

"Let me know what you think of this proposal," I ask. I'm a congenial guy at work, and people like me. I don't talk about myself much. My personal life is a bit of a mystery. I like it that way.

Toward the end of the day my colleague returns to my office. "Here's the proposal," he says, handing it back. "I made a few changes."

I tense. He made a few changes? What is he talking about? I know I asked him to make changes, I think to myself, but, I didn't want him to really make them. Who does he think he is?

"Thanks; I appreciate it." I say. I open the proposal, and I can't believe my eyes; red marks, fucking red marks! I commiserate with a coworker. "Can you believe this shit? Red marks!"

"Oh Tom, you've got to just let it go," she says. But I don't want to let it go.

Now several hours later, it still irritates the hell out of me. "Stupid prick; I'll show that little bastard," I think. The room is dimly lit. I like it that way. It's time for a drink. I like the ritual. I uncork the bottle, pour a small amount in a glass and give a sniff, as if I knew what I was looking for. I top off the glass and settle in for the evening in my lounge chair. I quickly finish off the glass and pour another. Ah, that's better; things start to quiet down. Screw that jerk. I'm just going to ignore his comments anyway. Life is good, and life is horrible.

"Smile." People are always telling me to smile as I walk down the halls at work. I smile politely.

"Smile yourself," I think to myself; what is there to smile about? My mind drifts to the past and to my incompetence at becoming successful, making more money, or having more of something, anything. Why can't I just be like this person or that person? A girlfriend. A nice girlfriend, that's what I need. Shoot, you know that's not going to happen. "I'm really not good enough for a "nice" girlfriend," I think to myself.

Something's missing and something is wrong with me. I see it as an article of faith. It's true because I say it's true. Out of someplace very dark, opaque, a familiar feeling wraps its arms around me. It reminds me of an express elevator that starts at my toes and ends at the top of my head. Where is this coming from? I'm overcome with despair; my eyes sink to the back of my head, and my jaw slackens.

I'm in a place that brings to mind an approaching storm, but ironically it's comfortable in its own way. Storms can be beautiful. I know what to expect from a storm. I used to be afraid of the lightening. Now I sometimes stand in front of the window watching it. A lump begins to form in my throat; it seems as if it had always been there. It's always near. I choke it off.

"*Damn,* I can't stand to cry. I do. I *hate* it. *Everyone* knows it's a sign of weakness." A tear rolls down my cheek. If I could just roll back the clock, I would do things differently, damn it. No. Jesus, I don't want to go back *there,* but I don't know of anyplace else to go. There is only the past and the future, and I fear the future and regret the past, but at least it's familiar. The present? There is no present. I pour another drink.

I'm on a downward spiral. I neither want nor do I need any help. That's for the weak. The phone rings; I don't answer it. I imagine a gun at my side. I imagine putting a bullet in the chamber and putting it to my head, and momentarily I feel some relief. There *is* a way out of this living hell. But I can't do that; I just can't. I am terrified of life and terrified of death. Maybe pills, I think to myself, a handful of pills and a bottle of wine or two would make me pass out and not wake up, maybe.

I enjoy being with people for short stretches, and then I need them to go away. People have a way of irritating me. "Alone is better," I tell myself, but it's self-sabotage. "You seem to do much better alone," my daughter tells me. She's right, but when you have a family, it makes for hard living. If only they were different, I tell myself. If only they were different.

I hear someone climb my steps, then a knock at the door. Terrific, who could that be? "I thought I'd surprise you," my girlfriend says with a smile. Big mistake. What in the hell gives her the right to interrupt my drinking time? This is my time, and I'm pissed. "Well Goddamn it, call first. Jesus, you can't just show up at my door without calling."

She's incredulous, confused as to why I would be acting that way. She looks at me as if I'd lost my mind. We argue. "Just get outta here," I tell her. She finally leaves in tears. Ah, who gives a shit? Good things don't last anyway. Good riddance. I feel guilty and ashamed. God, I'm a jerk. But damnit, she should have called first. Another drink and I don't feel so guilty and ashamed anymore. Screw it!

Anyway there won't be any surprises tonight. Tonight I'm alone, and that's okay. I guess its okay. I wonder if my friend is home. No, forget it; I don't want to talk with anyone. After a few more drinks the lump in my throat disappears, my eyes become heavy, and I doze off on the couch with the television on.

I have some very strict rules about drinking. No drinking before 5:00 PM on weekends and 6:00 PM on workdays. But I've cleverly devised a loophole. The loophole allows me to break the rules anytime I please. You only live once, and there are only 365 drinking days in the year. The next day I go to work and think about 6:00 PM. I'll need another bottle.

CHAPTER 3

Sometimes I just sit here in my small apartment with a drink, listening to music, staring into space. It's not long before I take that inevitable trip to the past. I constantly analyze the past. I look in its corners and crevasses for some clue to—I don't know what. I think of a time nearly thirty years ago. I think of some friends I had as a kid. I wonder about them from time to time and the things we did at The Shack. That's what we called it. Sometimes it makes me sad. So I pour another drink, and I hear Eddie Money sing, *"I wanna go back and do it all over."* "Jesus," I think. "Why would anyone want to do that?" Sometimes I do though, and I'm not sure why.

I believe that we are the sum total of what happens inside the womb and what happens outside the womb. How could it be any different? Some are born predisposed to behave in ways that others are not. They're wired that way. Not an excuse, but it could be. For me it could be useful. Some of us learn to express ourselves in healthy ways. I don't know how they do it. I seem to be very good at expressing myself in unhealthy ways. I'm an expert at anger, resentment, envy, and isolation.

"How do you train the dog to heel, Dad?" I asked.

"You take this leash and swat him on the ass like this," my father answered. The dog yelped and shook in fear. "Now you try it."

"But, why, Dad? I don't want to do it."

"It's how you get the dog to respect you. Now do it. Don't make me ask you again."

I feel sick to my stomach as I lamely hit the dog with the leash. "Goddamn it, not like that. Like this." The dog yelped again. The dog shook. My head was spinning. "Dad, I'm getting a headache."

Spike was a Labrador Retriever, a terrific hunting dog. He came along when I went pheasant or partridge hunting with my dad. Sometimes my grandfather would come with us. On a colorful fall afternoon we were walking back to the car after a day of hunting. "Never, ever, point a gun at someone unless you intend to shoot him," my dad would say. I was walking in front of my dad and grandfather.

In truth I was not all that thrilled about shooting birds, or anything else for that matter. This whole business was more about being outdoors, and today it felt good to be walking in the woods. My grandfather, I learned, had a somewhat bizarre, perhaps even twisted sense of humor. He placed the barrel of his twelve gauge shotgun six to twelve inches from my ear and slightly behind my head. I imagine he whispered in my dad's ear, "Watch Tom jump." He pulled the trigger, and I nearly came out of my skin. With my ears ringing I turned to find that they had played a joke on me.

Both of them thought it funny, but I was pissed. I didn't dare show it, though, so I played along. Better to do that than to voice my displeasure and risk punishment. I don't know whether that incident had anything to do with it, but loud noises still make me jump, and they make me angry.

Anyway, Spike had a large cage in the backyard. For hours and hours he paced around in circles. He beat down a path that reminded me of a race track. I felt bad for him. He was a good dog, and he needed to have some room to run, for crying out loud. On occasion he would get out of his cage, and I wished that he would run away, make his break for "freedom." My dad gave the dog away when he and my mom divorced. I was more happy than sad.

Dear Tom,

"Everybody line up for a lickin'," is what your dad used to say. That's what he called it. Not a spanking but a lickin'. For what? Well, it didn't matter. It could be because you'd disobeyed him, or it could be because he'd had a bad day at work. Anytime he had to say something more than once, it usually meant a "lickin'." The weapon of choice could be a paddle, a spatula, or his belt.

You remember a time when he was training one of your dogs. He'd walk that poor dog back and forth across the yard. When the dog didn't respond to an order, he'd take the leash and viciously hit the dog. The dog was clearly terrified. It was that way with you. When you wouldn't stop crying, he hit you in the mouth with the spatula. Your mouth bled. Your mom didn't know what to do.

So when you heard "Line up," your guts twisted. He'd ask who wanted to go first. Asking which one of you wanted to get a beating first seemed a bit perverted to you, even sadistic. He'd sit on the side of the bed, weapon in hand, and ask which one of you wanted to go first. You always volunteered to do it; let's just get this thing over with, you thought. So there was your father, sitting on the bed. You'd walk over, pull your pants down, and lie down across his lap. With your brothers looking on and your mom nearby, it began. Your mom seemed helpless to do anything about it.

But that wasn't the worst part. When it was over you heard the sound of the weapon on your brother's skin, and then the screams. It was the screams that bothered you the most. You could take the beatings, but please make those screams stop. What is that son of a bitch doing to them? Enough already! The screams, God, you hated the screams.

You simply didn't get it. Why, you wondered. Why would someone do that? How could someone do that? You saw a grin on your dad's face; was he really enjoying it? Could it be? No, it couldn't be. But it seemed that way.

You remember the smells in the house. You could never describe the smell—musty perhaps. It's the same smell as in your grandparents' house. You hate that smell.

You want to say something about the smell. You want to scream it: "This place stinks; make this smell go away. And about your shit-eating grin, wipe it off, and if you hit me or my brothers again, you're going to regret it." You wanted to scream it, and you were afraid of what you might do if you did. The anger welled up inside you, but there was no place to release it.

That's the hard cold truth isn't it? It's hard to say, I know.

Let's leave it there for now. We'll talk again whenever you're ready.

Take care, my friend.

Sometimes I wonder what it's like to feel at peace with oneself. What is it like to be confident? Not just acting confident, but I mean really being confident in oneself. Some people are able to socialize effortlessly and make friends easily. I don't particularly like those people; they talk too damned much, but I wish I could be like them. I'm not comfortable being me, but there's a cure for that, and it comes in a bottle. Most times though I prefer to crawl out of my skin.

"Hey, Mom, I'm learning how to write my name in cursive. Look!" Mom walked over and took a peek. She turned from the paper I had written on to look at me. Surely she would be proud of her son.

"You know what they say about people who write their name over and over again, don't you?"

"No, what do they say?" I asked with a smile.

"They say they are full of themselves."

I've been told that alcoholics are egomaniacs with inferiority complexes. That description seems to fit, except for the alcoholic part. But listen; don't think for a minute that you have anything over on me. You are better than me, and you are less than me. Why better? You drive a nicer car, you have a bigger house, you have nicer clothes, you have a better haircut, and you make more money than I do, and so on and so on. Clearly that's the truth of the matter, and I despise you for it. But let's be clear. You don't deserve the nice house and the nice car, I do. God screwed me out of that, though. Consider yourself lucky.

I've become quite the expert at self-loathing. There have been times when I thought that changing my name seemed like a good idea. I don't understand why, but I hated my name, and I sometimes pretended I had another, particularly when meeting people I'd probably never see again.

"Hi, what's your name?"

"Um, Ted."

"Ted, what?"

The name that came to mind was that of a former hockey player of the Detroit Red Wings. Harris. Ted Harris. Maybe I have something to hide. I don't know. Maybe I'm not supposed to feel good about myself. I suppose it's part wiring and part environment. Drinking was the antidote. Drinking made me feel better, and it made me feel normal. Living was easier, at least in the short term, and that's all that mattered most of the time. All the noise and the spinning in my head stopped, and I felt as if I could live with myself. With each drink my troubles become smaller and my future brighter. I had big, grandiose plans that came to fruition only in the bottom of a glass.

West Central Florida, 1999

If you really want to hear about it, the first thing you'll probably want to know is where I was born, and what my lousy childhood was like, and how my parents were occupied and all before they had me, and all that David Copperfield kind of crap, but I don't feel like going into it, if you want to know the truth.

—J. D. Salinger (1919–), *The Catcher in the Rye*

CHAPTER 4

How do I square serendipity with the will of God? I'm told that everything is the way it's supposed to be, that it's all part of God's plan. And God has a plan for me; I just need to accept it. Yet we do have serendipitous moments? How can that be? Is it part of God's plan, or is it just dumb luck? I can't square the two. I have a tendency to analyze things to death. Maybe that's part of my problem. Maybe I think too much.

Tonight, though, I'm tired. I'm just emotionally exhausted. Please God, take care of my kids, and please, please, don't let me wake up in the morning. I say this to myself before I sack out. It's a stretch to call it a prayer. Let's just say I've said it before—how may times I can't say. I do know it was many times. But I have a problem. I'm a certifiable coward. I don't have the balls to end my own life, so I often look for other ways to get it done.

Maybe God would do it if I asked nicely. Maybe he would see that I've had enough of life, or maybe he's not paying attention. I sometimes tell my wife that I wish someone would just come up from behind and shoot me; I'd laugh about it.

But it wasn't a joke. Riding my bike on the road I think, well, maybe today is the day I get hit by a car. I just don't want to see it coming. I wished I had the balls because, well, I didn't see any hope, only despair. I look for hope, but it can't be found in this life. Life is a cruel joke, and it's painful. Life can be unbearable. How do you tell your spouse the pain you are feeling? I don't, it sounds like whining. There are no visible signs of trauma; no cuts, no bruises, no proof. They're all on the inside.

I'm out on a long pier that extends into the ocean. It's a sunny day, and the water is a beautiful color, a turquoise blue, and so clear. At the very end of the pier there is a small shack. I look out the window of this shack at some children who are playing in the water. The kids are having a great time. Oh shit, oh shit. Is that a shark? Yeah, it's a shark. I yell at the kids to get out of the water. I beg them to get out of the water, but either they aren't listening or they can't hear me. This is bad. This is really bad. The children start to scream. I cover my ears and look toward a mirror that is hanging on the wall. I pray to God to make the screaming stop. To my horror, blood splatters on the mirror, and the screaming stops. I hate dreaming.

Poor, poor me. I'm depressed. Everyone has their share of troubles don't they? Maybe, just maybe, I would end my own life. It's not worth a nickel, but, my kids. I don't want to hurt them, and as that hackneyed phrase goes, I love them more than life. Oh shit, I think. A cliché is the best I can do? What parent doesn't love his or her kids more than life? Can't I do anything original? Guilt, shame, self-pity, depression—here it comes.

What the hell is going on? How did I get in here? I realize I'm up to my neck treading water. It's cold, and all around me it's dark, but I can make out the faint outline of brick. Yeah, it's brick. I'm overwhelmed with despair, and I start to weep. I want to let lose with a good cry, but I'm afraid of that. I look up and see a distant light. Is that a star? For a moment I think there might be some hope?

But I'm fooling myself because now I recognize that I'm in the bottom of a very deep well. This is the face of depression. This is what it's all about. I feel nothing but despair, sadness, a sense of overwhelming grief. It's dark. I'm afraid, but the fear turns to surrender. I can only tread water for so long. It gets old and I get tired—giving up seems to be the only option.

For me it's a familiar and oddly comfortable place. There's no light at the bottom of the well, and there's no hope of getting out. I'm trapped, and the only escape from this horrible situation is suicide. The thought of it lifts a burden from my shoulders; I feel better because there is a way out after all. There is hope, and it, too, has a face. But it can only be found at the expense of others. Goddamn it! I appreciate the impact of suicide on others. It's horrible, and I wish it weren't. Still, life is hard everyday. It sucks. Where the hell is God? What did he do, step out of the office? Didn't he hear me?

I make my way to the bathroom in the morning. "*Son of a bitch, I woke up again.*" I guess God wasn't paying attention after all. Fine then, maybe a drink or a pill will help. Yeah, it always helps.

Dear God,

"Seek and ye shall find," my mother used to tell me. It's right there in the Bible, I'm told. I don't know whether my mother ever found what she was seeking; perhaps she found it in death.

As for me, I'm seeking peace and happiness. I've looked for them in both material possessions and spirituality. I've had glimpses of both, only to have them taken away.

Twenty years ago I had an affair. I lost my family, my job, my mother—all within a couple of weeks. I was broke and terribly depressed. I thought that perhaps this was just punishment for the mistreatment of my family. Adultery is, after all, one of those 10 Commandment things. I had violated it, and it came with a hefty price. I apologized to you, got down on my knees, and begged for forgiveness—and it was about five years before I got back on my feet.

Here I am more than twenty years later, separated, broke, and depressed; perhaps the fine is one that can never be paid. I don't know. I hope this is not about taking some pills. Is that what this is about? Taking some pills?

Today I've settled on the way things are. I don't ask you for anything. I am reminded of your presence from time to time, but I have no expectations. I've put away the books, the ones that talk of worries going by the way, if only I would maintain my conscious contact with you. You see, I'm skeptical. I don't want to confuse serendipity with divine intervention. Fool me once, shame on you; fool me twice…well, you know how it goes.

"Faith without works is dead," they say. Maybe; maybe not. I kind of doubt it. I've put in my work. I've prayed. I've mediated. I've handed over my problems, my fears, and my life to you.

I think I've changed my mind; I want it back.

Maybe you are busy. You know of the problems we humans have. There's the little problem of war and genocide in the world, the family down the road with a terminally ill relative, perhaps a parent with a child who has committed suicide, I understand my problems pale in comparison. I'm almost embarrassed that you would give me the time of day. You have a lot to do.

Here's the vexing and troubling concern, and why I'm more disillusioned than angry. I've been told that you want all of us, regardless of the magnitude of our troubles, to be happy, joyous, and free. The directions for getting there are simple. Just twelve simple steps. I believed that. I did that, but I'm not happy, joyous, and free.

I'm not going to have a hissy fit over it—been there; done that. But I'm not going to pick up a book and read how great things might be—been there, done that.

Happy, joyous, and free, huh? Well, I hope you'll forgive me, but I'm dubious.

Best,

Tom

PS. You, no doubt can sense the self-pity sprinkled throughout this letter. It's true of course. But I've decided that today I'm not going to feel guilty about it. Today I think I'll just ride with it.

West Central Florida, 2004

The greatest mistake you can make in life is to continually fear you will make one.

—Elbert Hubbard (1856–1915)

CHAPTER 5

"I need to confront you about something." Oh, for the love of Christ, what did I do now? I don't want to be "confronted." Not today. Not any day, really. I don't even like that word; it's too. I don't know—clinical. I'd rather have someone get right to the point—let's get the bad news over with.

"Okay, Tom you fucked up!" The quicker the better. C'mon, out with it. But I never say that. Maybe I'd hurt their feelings. Besides, I'm a nice guy. Waiting a few seconds only serves to heighten my anxiety. Only my therapist and my wife would use a word like "confronted." She missed her calling. Where, oh where, did I screw up now?

I leaned back in the chair, a little intimidated, and a little unsure of what I was about to hear. But I'm keeping my cool. I remember that old line. "Never let 'em see you sweat." Don't show any emotion one way or the other, I always say. Better to keep them guessing than to show your hand. Stoicism is virtue. "Okay," I replied. "I need to ask you about the pain pills you've been taking." Oh *shit!* A buzz went through my body. I had just been busted.

A few months earlier, my wife and I had had our second child, Sarah, the youngest of three girls. My first had been from a previous marriage and was now going to college. My wife had been prescribed Oxycodone for pain. I knew she was going to get *something* for pain. What would be prescribed really didn't make any difference to me. It wasn't my "drug of choice," alcohol was, so taking some really wouldn't constitute a relapse. Not to me anyway. It didn't take a lot of self-talk to convince myself of that. A thought flashed through my mind. I think of an AA meeting where someone says "Hello, my name is Bob, and I'm an alcoholic and an addict." What the *hell* is the difference I think—alcohol *is* a drug, Einstein. *Jesus,* some people really irritate me. I feel the need to set this person straight. What an *asshole!*

My drinking begins at 5:00 PM on the dot, and I usually pass out no later than 9:00 PM. I wake up at 6:00 AM or so, worry about my lack of success at starting a home business, start drinking at 5:00 PM again (worrying takes a lot out of me), and I pass out by 9:00 PM. Our first child was just a baby, and she woke up crying somewhere around 10:00 PM. My wife was tired and needed help. She wasn't getting any from me. No sir, it was *her* fault that I was unemployed, and it was *her* fault we were broke; she was just getting what she deserved.

"Tom, Tom. I need some help." she said, holding our crying child. What's the problem? Can't she see I'm passed out?

"*No!*" I hollered back. The crying continued from my wife and from the baby. I can't sleep through all this noise. I finally get up agitated and disgusted. "*Goddamn it,*" I muttered. "Here, *give her to me,*" I demanded. The baby's crying became louder.

She was scared. Why was she scared, and why wouldn't my wife give Catherine to me? My wife's eyes got bigger, and her voice changed. She seemed to be in a panic and afraid. "Why," I wondered. "What in the hell is she acting like that for?" She called the police. The *police,* for Christ's sake! I needed to quit drinking for good this time.

So here I was, five years later. The bottle of pain medication was on the nightstand. I looked in its direction once, then again. I picked it up, brought it up to my face, and then put it back on the nightstand. I scratched my head and looked around. No one was home. What the hell was I worried about? Jesus, why am I being so paranoid, this is ridiculous. Tom. You're just being silly! She wouldn't notice if I had just one lousy, stinking pill, would she? Hell, no. Besides, I have a headache; yeah, a headache. I get these temple-busting headaches all the time. These damned things just won't go away with over-the-counter medication!

I've thought this through, and I believe I have made a reasonable argument. I just gave myself a good logical reason to have one, just one, lousy pain pill for this nasty headache of mine. Why is it I feel guilt about this? God, my headache hurts! Thank goodness, reasoning is one of my strong points. My reasoning was evidently flawed. It didn't stop at one; it never did. And over a matter of days, a bottle full of pills had been reduced to just one. That's a problem: just one pill left in the bottle. They don't last forever. How could I get more? Let's see here; is there a refill? No refill. Damn.

Over time I somehow manage to convince myself that she wouldn't notice that the entire bottle was all but gone. Her silence reinforced that notion. I suppose leaving one pill is akin to leaving just a swallow in the bottom of a bottle. It provides a kind of plausible deniability. "Tom, you drank the whole bottle!"

"No, that's not true; see, there's still some left." There was a time when I would limit myself to the proverbial two glasses of wine. I had discussed my "problem" with my wife, and I had agreed to no more than two glasses per day. Why two? I don't know; it's always two isn't it?

"How much have you had to drink this evening, sonny?" "Um. Let's see, just a couple of beers, officer." "Just the two beers, huh?" "Yeah, honest, just the two." I suppose one seems completely unbelievable, and three seems like "real drinking." So two was the magic number, and two it would be. My wife brought home a bottle and put it on the counter. I looked at the bottle and then looked at her, a bit bewildered. Why isn't she opening that? I mean, who just walks away from a nice bottle of wine? "Aren't you going to open it?" I inquired.

"Not right now," she replied walking away. I looked at the clock; it was 5:00 PM. What is she talking about, "not right now?" I'm getting a little antsy now. A couple of minutes pass; that's enough. "I'm gonna go ahead and open it; do you want a glass?" "No, maybe later," she says. "Fine by me," I think.

I told myself I had control over alcohol, while at the same time I devised schemes to ensure an ample supply. So I came up with a way around the two-glass-limit I had imposed on myself. I cleverly made sure I had a very, very large glass. Top it off, take a drink, and top it off again. It's both funny and pathetic. It worked very well though. I managed to polish off an entire bottle in two glasses—except for a swallow. While two was the goal, it was never enough, of course. I can handle more than two, but how the hell am I going to get around this self-imposed limit? I should have never agreed to it in the first place.

Sometimes I know how to really screw up my life, I think. Can I hide a bottle outside? Wait a minute; I think I've figured this problem out. What if I suggested take-out for dinner? There's a place just down the street with a nice wine list. Yeah, that way I could sit at the bar and have a couple while waiting for dinner. That, plus the two at home—"*Jesus,* it's brilliant!" "How about some take-out for dinner?" I ask.

"Again?" she says. "I'll go get it; how about it? I'll just run down and pick up some dinner." I'm almost pleading.

"Well. Okay, I guess." This was going to work. But people do notice. I mean, how many nights per week does a family have take-out. At the same place? My plan was transparent. I thought I had pulled off a brilliant maneuver. My wife never said a word, but she knew what I was up to.

So an hour or so later, she walked into the kitchen to pour a glass for herself. She picked up the bottle and noticed just a swallow in the bottom. "How many glasses did you have?" she asked looking at the bottle. "Just two." I answered. "You had just *two* glasses?" The only person I had fooled was myself.

At the time I was taking the Oxycodone, and, unknown to anyone else, I had stopped taking the prescribed antidepressants that I had been taking for years. This turned out to be a very bad decision. I was diagnosed with depression, which had always made for dramatic writing, in a good sense, and dramatic living, in a lousy sense. Ironically I was eager to take medication that wasn't prescribed for me, but I refused to take the medication that was.

I was going on six years of sobriety, and it all came to an end when I took the first pill. That, and a history of unresolved issues (doesn't everybody have issues?), put me squarely on the road to insanity. If only I had recognized it sooner. Truthfully it wouldn't have made any difference if I had.

The Shack, 1968–69

Friends have all things in common.

—Plato (427 BC–347 BC), *Dialogues, Phaedrus*

CHAPTER 6

Life started when I was thirteen or fourteen. I don't remember much before then. The following five years or so are indelibly etched in my mind. Some memories I'd just as soon forget, while others are to be cherished. I wish I could put some of the photos I have in my head onto paper. Memorable things happened around that point in my life, some good and some bad, and I often think about them. Martin Luther King Jr. and Robert Kennedy had been assassinated.

I remember the march that MLK had led in Memphis the day before. I remember seeing on the news the speech Bobby Kennedy had made in Los Angeles just before he was killed. I cried in private when Bobby Kennedy was killed. The war in Vietnam, of course, led off the news every night. My dad supported it, my mom didn't; but she didn't talk much about it. My dad explained to me over and over that the United States had "never lost a war, and we won't lose this one either."

There were riots in Chicago and elsewhere. They scared the hell out me. I was certain the riots would one day come to our white, middle-class doorstep, up to my bedroom, where I would get the shit beaten out of me. I needed a plan. My dad, though, was happy to see that those "Damned hippies" in Chicago finally get what was coming to them. Stinking long-hairs needed to be put on the path of a good crew cut, Goddamn it, and, by the way, as long as I lived in the house, my hair was going to be short, "and I mean *short*," my dad would say.

Then a few years later I was able I let my hair grow past my shoulders. It was a time when wearing the flag was a sign of protest rather than a sign of patriotism. It was a time when my parents decided to go through a messy divorce. Shoot, everyone in the neighborhood was having some sort of crisis. People were having affairs, airing their dirty laundry in public, leaving their husbands, wives, and kids. Given the frequency of occurrence, you might think that arguing with each other and public drunkenness were faddish. It seemed to me that it couldn't possibly be any other way. The neighborhood I grew up in epitomized that trite, yet accurate, term, *dysfunctional*. Hell, it should have been a TV series.

There was the knock at the door. It was 1996, and my dad was showing up for dinner. My dad had been sober for thirty years. His second wife had left him for another guy. He was really doing very well. "Let's have him over for a Sunday meal," my wife suggested. So we sat down at the table, and the conversation turned to years past. My dad talked often of the past. I tensed.

"You know, I was kind of rough on you during my drinking days."

"Yeah. You were," I said without looking up.

"I suppose they would consider it child abuse today." He chuckled lightly.

"Yeah, I think they would." There was silence as we continued to eat. Finally, the silence was broken.

"You're never going to forgive me for that are you?"

I looked at my plate, still chewing my food. "Nope."

Maybe it was just the gang I hung out with, but there seemed to be a lot of that going around when I was a kid. Beatings, drinking, fighting. It was normal. Wasn't it normal?

In the late 60s, Ralphie, Mitch, Jake, and I found some comfort in one another. Maybe we became such good friends because we had so much in common. We laughed with each other, fought with each other, and stood up for each other. Girls, we discovered had breasts. Alcohol, we discovered, made us feel large. It helped us forget our problems, if only temporarily. It also emboldened us to do things we wouldn't otherwise do. Like talk to girls.

And that's what life was all about. Girls and alcohol were and still are the common thread among young boys—and among old men. Growing up was not a possibility. We were going to stay young forever. In the summer of 1969, at fourteen years old, I had my first blackout from drinking too much. It's really a miracle I lived through that. There are days when I wish I hadn't. It was my first blackout; but it would not be my last. My adolescence had taken a detour, and I believe I stopped growing emotionally. In other ways, I was old beyond my years. So much for staying young forever. Some light drinking soon metastasized into routine drunkenness.

West Michigan, Late Spring, 1969

When someone allows you to bear his burdens, you have found deep friendship.

—Unknown

CHAPTER 7

The last class of the day, of the week, and of this particular school year was ninth grade Civics. It was always a good class to end the week with because, well, frankly, we didn't have to do shit in this class. To the demise of Henry Albertson's mental health and eventually of his job, every troublemaker and every smart-ass in the ninth grade was in that class.

Henry Albertson, HAWK, which stood for Henry Albertson Woman Killer, was a middle-aged, short, and portly man who wore large, round, and thick glasses. Where he picked up the nickname, I don't know, but he was rather proud of it, as he had it spelled out on his Plymouth Barracuda. Henry just didn't look right behind the wheel of a Barracuda. Imagine Pee Wee Herman on a Harley—the imagery just doesn't work.

"As you know," Mr. Albertson said, "I'm proud of the name; after all I've got it on my car. But I ask that you don't call me Hawk in class."

"Okay, Hawk," someone would reply.

Henry just shrugged his shoulders. He couldn't lecture because of the constant talking in class. He was simply unable to get anyone to shut up, so he thought that showing movies every day would solve the problem. It didn't. When the lights went out, everything from chewing gum to lug nuts to fresh fruit would be thrown at the screen. The gum usually stuck to the screen, the lug nut ripped right through, and a direct hit by a tangerine would result in the movie screen scrolling back up. Zip!

Hawk would stop the movie, turn on the lights, and insist that the perpetrator come forward. Sure. The problem was that there were several perpetrators: about half the class. "C'mon, Hawk, show the stinking movie. We won't do it again."

"All right, if you promise," he'd say. "Yeah, yeah, we promise." We were not all that good about keeping our promises, though. The final straw came when my buddy Mitch lit a firecracker in the back of the room. Under normal circumstances a firecracker exploding in a classroom might lead to panic, perhaps even to chaos. It might even result in a call to the police, and it would certainly end in expulsion. But not in this class.

A flash was followed by a loud bang. Again, off with the movie projector, on with the lights. "People, please. We simply *can't* go on like this. You know we can't go on like this." Hawk pleaded and begged.

Mitch, being an eleven on the smart-ass scale of one to ten chimed in, "You're right, Henry. I think we should call off the marriage." The class exploded in laughter.

Hawk showed his displeasure and utter inability to control the class by first standing for a few seconds in stunned silence. This was usually followed by the cupping of his hands over his mouth as if he were about to vomit in them. Then he walked briskly out of the room.

He returned to the classroom after about ten minutes or so. Slowly he walked, bent over, to his desk. He looked beaten. He dabbed his mouth with a handkerchief. He'd start to say something when one of the smart-asses would raise his hand.

"Yes, Tom." "Well, we were all just taking bets. Half of us say you were throwing up; the other half says you were masturbating. Who's right?"

Dead quiet. We had thrown various and sundry objects at the movie screen, and we had thrown insults at the teacher and at each other, but nobody had every used the "M" word before. The calm was broken.

"Yeah," another smart-ass shouted. "Are you or are you not a master debater?" For fourteen-year-olds that was a funny line. The room once again exploded in laughter. Exit Hawk with his hands over his mouth.

During tests someone would invariably ask him for a hint, as Hawk could easily be manipulated into giving the answer. "Hawk, how many senators are there anyway?"

"You know I can't tell you that," he'd say.

"Aw, c'mon; give us a hint."

Others in the class would weigh in. "Just one hint. C'mon, Hawk, just one lousy hint."

"Uh. Oh, all right. There are—uh—two senators for each state." Since most of us were dumbasses on top of being smart-asses, we'd press on. He finally caved. "All right, all right," his voice rising, "there are one hundred senators, two for each state. There are fifty states, for the love of Pete! Can't you people do the math?"

We probably couldn't, but he was proud of that one. He had a grin that reminded me of the Cat in the Hat. I think I noticed the corners of his mouth curl upward, and I actually felt good that he got one in. But we got our answers, and all of us, through a miracle referred to as the "Get these people the hell out of my life" miracle, passed the class. The obvious truth was he didn't want to see us in a classroom again. And he never did. He was fired.

I felt bad about it, and it occupied my mind for a long time. No one seemed to care, though. I don't know what ever happened to him, but on occasion he would be seen driving through town in his white Barracuda with Hawk written on the side in metal-flake letters.

As we left school, a friend, Steve Flanagan, flagged us down. "You guys interested in some weed?" We stopped, and he approached, reached in his pocket, and pulled out a baggy with oregano.

"Lemme see that," I said as I looked over the "weed."

Steve's parents had a kind of loft in their garage. We spent our time up there smoking cigarettes and drinking beer. One of our classmates, Lisa Bellows, an attractive girl, joined us. Steve and Ralphie were hell bent on running away, and they were trying to convince Lisa to go with them. "I'll take care of you," Steve pleaded, waving a cigarette around.

Ralphie did one better. "Just tell me what you want. Whatever you want; I'll buy it for you." I leaned against the wall, thinking these guys were nuts. Lisa wasn't buying it either. Somehow word of their plan made its way to Ralphie's mom. She tracked down Steve and Ralphie about a mile from the loft, and their little adventure came to an abrupt end. They had been carrying a grocery bag with soda, beer, cigarettes, and an assortment of junk food. Steve held on to the groceries, and Ralphie got a chewing out.

Anyway, after inspecting the weed, I exchanged glances with Jake, Mitch, and Ralphie. "How much did you pay for this?"

Steve looked around to make sure that he wasn't overheard by a "narc." Of course every new kid had been suspected of being a "narc."

"Five bucks. You wanna buy some?"

Mitch responded for all of us. "You just spent five dollars on a bag of oregano, dumbass!" Steve snatched it from my hands and held it up to his face. He shook the bag, looked at it some more, then opened it and gave it a sniff. "Well *Goddamn!*" he said, stomping around. He suddenly stopped as though he had come up with a bright idea. "What do you think I could sell it for?" Not such a bright idea.

"A dime," said Ralphie. "Listen, Steve, we're going to drink a few beers if you want to come down." I started off. Jake chimed in with perhaps the most important question of the day. "Oh really? Where are we gonna get this beer you're talking about?"

"C'mon; you know. The Shack, remember?" I asked. Everyone looked at me. waiting for the answer. "Jesus, c'mon. We've got about eight or nine beers left down by The Shack."

"That's right. I forgot about that," said a suddenly more upbeat Jake. "Okay, we'll see you guys around seven." Ralphie walked west, and the three of us—Mitch, Jake, and I walked east. Steve went about trying to peddle his bag of oregano. He convinced some numb nuts that if he bought the bag for five dollars he could turn it around and sell it for ten.

West Michigan, Early Summer, 1969

Happy families are all alike; every unhappy family is unhappy in its own way.

—Leo Tolstoy (1828–1910), *Anna Karenina*

CHAPTER 8

I was in the backyard with the dog when my dad hollered out the door, "Tom, phone." I ran inside and picked up the receiver. "Hello." It was Ralphie. "You got to come over here man! Mrs. Pinter is lying in her backyard."

My eyes widened. "No kidding?"

"No kidding, Mitch is over here too."

"What are you guys doing?" I asked.

"What do you think? Are you going to come over here or not?" Mrs. Pinter was *the* divorcee on our block. Oh, there were others that I used to watch from the garage roof with a pair of binoculars. Mrs. Pinter, though, was definitely everyone's fantasy. She lived just behind Ralphie's house across the alley. And she had a body that was well-proportioned. There were bushes along the fence that separated her yard and the alley, but one could easily see over and between them. Watching Mrs. Pinter was a hobby I shared with many others, and an alarm went off in the neighborhood when she was in the backyard.

After hanging up the phone, I ran out the back door, opened the gate to our fence, took a right-hand turn in the alley, and saw Ralphie and Mitch crouched down about a block away, looking through the bushes. They saw me and waved me ahead. I crouched down as I slowly approached. "What is she wearing?" I whispered. "A bikini," a giddy Ralphie whispered back.

"Let me see!" I looked through the bushes, and there she was, lying on her back on a beach towel. "Man, she has some big knockers." Mitch wasn't saying much, as he was busy trying to focus his binoculars.

"I bet I could talk her into screwing," Ralphie boasted.

I looked Ralphies way.

"Okay," Ralphie continued, "*maybe* I could talk her into it."

Then Mitch broke in. "Holy *shit,*" he whispered, "we got pubic hair. I can see some pubic hair." We looked through the binoculars and sure enough, there was pubic hair, the holy grail of voyeurism. While we continued to stare in awe at Mrs. Pinter, my brother had come down the alley, unnoticed by any of us. He had stopped in front of the fence and just behind us.

"Tom, Dad wants you to come home now." We nearly jumped out of our skin, but we didn't make a sound. Mrs. Pinter looked toward my brother. "Hi, Mrs. Pinter." "Hello, Richard. Say hello to your brother for me." "He's right here, Mrs. Pinter," he said pointing toward the bushes.

"Yeah, I know where he is." I contemplated the ways I was going to kick my brother's ass. *I* could kick his ass, but nobody else could. Ralphie learned that when he started shoving my brother around one day. "Ralphie. Leave my brother alone, man." He kept shoving my brother around. "Ralphie, I'm not kidding around here," I said. I was getting quite pissed. Still Ralphie continued to shove my brother. That was enough. I threw a right hand that landed squarely on Ralphie's nose, and down he went.

"*Goddamn it, Tommy,* you broke my fucking nose. Jesus Christ, man!" Ralphie walked home holding his hand to his bloody nose, hurling an occasional insult my way. His nose wasn't broken, but he never picked on my brother again. That was my job. It took Ralphie about twenty-four hours to forget the incident and we were buddies again. So anyway I went home, hoping that Mrs. Pinter would not say anything to my parents. She didn't.

My dad is a recovering alcoholic. If you had known him in the late sixties and early seventies, you wouldn't recognize him today. He is a different and better man. He is kind and soft spoken. On the day he admitted himself to the hospital, he had just a few dollars in his pocket, and he was hallucinating, swatting at imaginary flies. Sprawled out on the kitchen floor and unable to function, he asked to be taken to the hospital. In the late 60's his alcoholism was in full bloom. He had booze in the garage, in the shed, in the boat, and under the car seat.

"Settles my stomach," he'd say, taking a swig of vodka followed by some Pepto-Bismol. He drank vodka because he believed no one would be able to smell the booze on his breath. His parents (my grandparents) were also alcoholics, although they never recognized their alcoholism. My grandfather would never do that. He never believed my dad had a drinking problem. Even after Dad dried out in the hospital, he offered him drinks. He could be a son of a bitch.

My brothers are also recovering alcoholics. My mother couldn't handle booze very well, and she was clinically depressed, whatever that means.

Ralphie and I are sitting in my bedroom listening to the Beatles' Sgt Pepper's Lonely Hearts' Club Band on an old record player of mine. We play "With a Little Help from my Friends" over and over again. My mother abruptly opens the door and walks in. She's pissed about something. She picks up my albums I had been collecting since 1963 or so, brings them up over her head, and throws them to the floor, where they shatter. Pieces of vinyl go all over my bedroom floor. As quickly as she enters, she leaves. Ralphie and I stare at each other with our mouths open.

Finally, Ralphie breaks the silence. "Shit! What's the matter with your mom?"

"I don't know man. I don't know."

Some time after the divorce, my mom married another alcoholic, who is now in recovery. There seems to be a pattern here. When my parents finally and mercifully divorced, I moved in with my dad, who had moved back in with his parents—the alcoholic son living with the alcoholic parents. Not exactly Ozzie and Harriet. My mom, my brothers, and her new husband Jack had moved out of town in 1971 and into a very large house on a lake. There they had a big yard, a boat, and lots of stuff to do—it was a terrific place for kids.

But I wanted to stay near my friends, and I just felt a bond with my dad. Frankly, I felt sorry for him. So I decided to move in with my dad and my grandparents—a not-so-terrific place for kids. It wasn't the best choice, but there were really no good ones. He and I moved into his old room, the room he had had as a kid. I didn't think about it at the time, but that must have been a terrible blow to his ego. After thirteen or fourteen years to have to move back in with your parents—well, if that's not an excuse to drink, then what is? My twin bed was next to his.

Before going to bed he put a can of Blatz beer on the nightstand that separated our beds. "A little something to get me going in the morning," he would say. He would also bring up a can of Seven-Up for me. What was a can of Seven-Up supposed to do for me, I thought.

Dad lifted furniture all day, so he asked me to put some Ben-Gay on his back before going to bed. He had also broken his hand. He claimed that he had dropped furniture on it, but rumor had it that the injury was the result of a bar fight. I don't know the real story. Anyway, rubbing Ben-Gay on my dad's back was not first on my list of most favorite things to do. I hated it. There was the smell of booze in the air; seemingly seeping from the pores in his skin. And then, of course, there was the smell of Ben-Gay. The combination was sickening.

That was the ritual. And every night my grandparents went through their ritual—their Miller High Life ritual. You could set your watch by it. At 6:45 PM, my grandmother started to fidget in her chair. At 6:50 PM, she continued to fidget, but she also started to lick her lips and look at her watch every few seconds. At 7:00 PM she got out her chair, walked over to my grandfather, and rubbed his back for about five minutes. Afterward he got up from his chair, walked into the kitchen wearing a white tank top, boxer-shorts, and long black socks. It seemed he always had the same thing on.

He returned with a couple of bottles of Miller High Life, a Coke, and potato chips on a serving tray. It was a grand event, and my grandmother could hardly contain herself. This happened night after night, and it never happened one minute before 7:00 PM. My grandmother watched the clock as if she were counting down to the New Year. "I got 7:00 o'clock, James," she would say.

"I got two minutes to," he would reply.

She looked at her watch again; then she looked back at him. "Oh, c'mon, James," she'd say in all seriousness.

"Two more minutes," he'd reply. I think he did it just to drive my grandmother crazy. He nearly succeeded. He was a control freak. Grandmother grew up in a Catholic home, but Gramps wouldn't let her go to a Catholic church. Nope...the Pope didn't know what he was talking about, and "no wife of mine is going to a Catholic church!" It didn't matter that she was raised in a Catholic home; that's just the way it was. His oldest son (my uncle) went to Notre Dame. I loved the irony.

"What's for dinner tonight, Mom?" I asked. "We're having liver and cauliflower." I tensed up. I hated cauliflower! It literally made me sick to my stomach. Not that liver did anything for me, but my dad loved liver and onions—and cauliflower. My dad was an intimidating figure at the table. He sat down at the head of the table with his elbows on it; something we were not allowed to do. In one hand he had his fork, in the other a slice of buttered bread. He always had the slice of bread. After he cut his meat, he stabbed a piece of the liver with his fork, put it into his mouth, followed by a bite of bread, and then washed it all down with a swallow of beer. He repeated the process over and over again.

For some reason the bite of bread always bugged the crap out of me. "Just eat your damned liver without the bread," I imagined myself saying. The cauliflower came my way. "No cauliflower for me," I said, thinking that maybe he wouldn't notice. He noticed.

"Take some cauliflower," my dad insisted. "You should be grateful you're getting any food at all." I took some, but it wasn't enough. He added more to my plate. I tried to eat it and gagged. "You're going to eat that Goddamned cauliflower."

"But it makes me sick," I said.

"You're not leaving the table until you clean off your plate." He took another bite of liver, followed by the bread and then the beer. "We're not wasting good food as long as there are starving people in the world."

"How does eating something that makes me gag help world hunger?" I thought. I sat there for an hour, then for another hour. I squirmed in my chair. Then my dad got impatient and threatened me with a belt unless I cleaned off my plate. "You've got five minutes to clean off that plate." I ate the cauliflower as fast as I could and then promptly threw it up. I haven't had cauliflower or liver in over thirty years.

My dad admits that he was never big on education. I suppose he was raised that way. He found other things rewarding, but education wasn't one of them. A C on my report card was good enough. College was out of the question anyway, so why bother busting a nut for an A? He never cared much for reading either. "Don't bother buying me any books or magazines," he'd say. "I'll never read the damn things anyway."

I read, though. I read books and articles from the stacks of Reader's Digest my grandparents had. It was a kind of escapism for me. My dad believed you graduated from high school and got a job; that's just the way things were done. That's what his father had done. White collar jobs were for pencil pushers. *Real men* were either manual laborers or in the military.

And that's what he wanted for me, in addition to a short haircut. Always that short haircut. When he was drinking, my hair seemed to bother him all the more. "I know some guys that will hold you down while I cut that Goddamned hair," he would say. Men went out at night with their buddies, hung out at the bar, and told stories, albeit slightly if not completely embellished. A barstool, someone to commiserate with, and a cold drink—shoot, what more could anyone want? My dad took me to those bars, where I sat for hours drinking Coke after Coke. Seemed like the thing to do. I liked being with my dad at the bar. It's funny though, no one else took his kid to the bar, or at least no one that I knew of.

"Hey, buddy; it's time to wake up. Got to go to work." It was 2:00 AM on Sunday morning. My dad made extra money by cleaning up a bar after closing. He asked if I wanted to go with him. I felt an obligation of sorts to go, so I did.

This particular establishment was hardcore. People were still sitting around the bar, finishing their drinks and smoking cigarettes. The smell was overpowering. I recall the patrons looking disheveled and haggard like the characters in *Barfly*. I could sleep on a cot in the back room for a couple of hours. Then around 4:00 or 5:00 AM, I'd wake up and help him. I felt bad for my dad. I wished that he didn't have to work so hard for a living.

Dear Dad,

There's an old saying that goes "Like father, like son."

I was determined that would not come to fruition. It was a lock——it just wasn't going to happen. There was a time when there was nothing about you I liked. Nothing. I couldn't see the positive for all the negative.

Those were bad years. And those were good years. You expected things from me that I didn't deliver. They were really, things that I didn't want to deliver. A star football player, a marine with a crew cut, an outdoorsman, a hunter, a camper——that's what you wanted me to be. When I was able you'll recall I grew my hair just as long as I could and quit football. I really didn't particularly like camping either, and, as for hunting, I was not really into shooting animals.

That seemed to piss you off, and you wondered out loud about my masculinity. "What do you got down there? Is some girl gonna find some balls or a pussy?" Real men, men with balls, I guess, do those things. I didn't. That and the long hair, well, let's just say it didn't go over very well. And what would others think about you? A son with hair past his shoulders? No way. "Here's five dollars; now get that Goddamned hair cut, or I'll cut it for you."

You didn't like what you saw. I didn't quite fit into your plans so you attempted to control me through intimidation. That's the problem with alcoholics like us. We want to control everything, even the things we have no control over. And truthfully we don't have control over anything. And then there was the physical abuse and the emotional abuse. Not once, not twice, but more times than I care to remember. Here's the truth: at one point I didn't care whether you lived or died. I really didn't. Do you remember the roughly two-and-a-half years that we didn't speak? No one wants to be controlled, particularly by abusive means. When given the chance, people opt to escape. I took that option.

But I've had an epiphany of sorts. All these years later I've come to realize that it was your disease, alcoholism, which was at the core of your problems. I need to separate you, the person, from the disease. You see I have the same disease.

You went through that rather ugly divorce; mom had an affair, and a child resulted. She lied to you. She said it wasn't yours. I overheard that conversation. You two were in the kitchen. I was in bed. It made me sick. I felt bad for you, and for me. I could see the pain in your face for a long time after that. There was not much that was good about that time. Many nights I went to sleep with clenched fists, and you gently pried them open before moving out of the house. It was gut-wrenching. We, my brothers and I, were caught in the crossfire. Parents should know better.

I recall a time at Christmas, shortly after you and mom divorced. You were living with Gramps and Grandma. You made each of us an ice fishing box out of plywood, designed to double as a seat. You had tacked a piece of carpet onto the seat. Inside the box there were an ice fishing pole, a few bobbers, some hooks, and so on. You couldn't afford much more. I know that killed you. I could see it in your eyes. You wore emotions on your face. I felt badly for you. But let me say that I appreciated that just about more than anything else I received that year. Perhaps more than anything since.

You wanted desperately to be a good father. You were around to play catch with, to shoot hockey pucks at, to sit in the back yard and look at the stars together (I liked that), and for those glorious sips of beer—always Blatz beer. Those were father and son moments. Those are the times I wanted to be like my Dad. I loved those times.

Well, here I am, many years later. I'm once divorced, I have three kids just like you do, and now I'm separated, broke, and having a problem with alcohol.

Oh, sure, we have our differences, and I'm beginning to realize that, despite our foibles, we're still good people. You're a good dad, and I'm a good son—not perfect by any stretch, but working toward it. We both have our inner demons; we both have alcoholism. Maybe we have more in common than I thought.

"Like father, like son," they say.

Best,

Tom

West Michigan, Summer, 1969

To fear love is to fear life, and those who fear life are already three parts dead.

—Bertrand Russell (1872–1970), *Marriage and Morals*

CHAPTER 9

Vernon Williams was a first class bullshitter. I was good at spotting bullshitters, maybe because I was a pretty good one myself. He steadfastly insisted that the Plymouth was the best car ever made. Of course his parents had one, a Plymouth Fury wagon, and maybe that had something to do with it.

"Vern, c'mon man, you're full of it. Are you telling me your mom's Plymouth station wagon is a better than a Ford?"

"It's not my mom's station wagon; it's my dad's station wagon, and yes, it's the best car in the world."

"Jesus, Vern, you really need to get out more. You're just being an idiot."

My dad had a Ford; my grandparents had Fords, that's the way it was. I liked Fords. Vern liked Plymouths. We debated the issue at least once a week.

There in Vern's backyard was a tree house the kids in the neighborhood had helped build. The tree house was well furnished with things such as the crates we used as shelves to hold cigarettes and food. It also had an old, torn-up reclining chair that was about half in and half out of the tree house, and an old car seat we had somehow gotten up there.

"You kids are going to fall right out of that chair someday and break your heads wide open," Vern's mom would tell us. But Vern assured her that it was "engineered to prevent that from happening." This was a place where we could meet, engage in some light petting with the neighborhood tart, and relax with a smoke. I couldn't stand to inhale, and I never took up smoking, but I could be cool enough just holding onto one. Why we took the cigarettes out of the package, put them in a jar and buried them, I don't know. But that's what we did. We buried everything we were not supposed to have. Cigarettes, beer, nudie magazines—we buried them. We also buried the legendary case of vodka down by The Shack.

"The Shack isn't just a place to hang out," Vern was fond of saying. "It's a way of life, kind of like the Hell's Angels."

I was incredulous. "Vern, what are you talking about? The Hell's Angels?"

"There are members of The Shack scattered all over the country!" he exclaimed. "It's incorporated, you know."

"Shack, Inc.?" I replied sarcastically.

"That's right; like I said, it's a way of life." I tried to ignore him and watch the little league baseball game, but there was no way to stop Vern once he got cranked up. "And there's something else you should know." He continued, "There's one thing members of The Shack never, ever joke about."

I took the bait. "And what would that be?" "You never joke about getting caught by your parents smoking. Never."

"Jesus! All right, Vern. I won't tell your mom and dad about your smoking habit."

"Okay, fine then. Don't believe me. Do it," he said, "and you'll be banned for life from The Shack."

I just shook my head. "Who's gonna ban me?"

Vern seemed to be caught off guard, but he recovered quickly. "The board." This can't get any dumber can it? Actually it probably could and probably did.

Down by Mueller's Lake there was a softball diamond. My dad played there during the summers. He was a good athlete, and it was fun to watch him. I was proud of my dad. With his jet black hair and blue eyes, he was a handsome guy by most any standard. He was artistic and athletic. Our sitter actually expressed some interest in him. She was fifteen. He told her that any interest was probably misplaced. Anyway, he had had opportunities to go to art school, but he had passed on them to manage a grocery store that his father had managed before him.

He was fired in late 1967. He sued for wrongful discharge and won. After that he worked as a manual laborer for the rest of his life. He didn't have a lot of money, but it didn't matter; he was my dad. Softball in the summer was as much about friends having a beer together as it is about the game, maybe more so. The game was a convenient and socially acceptable excuse to drink. My dad had a lot of buddies who enjoyed having a beer—or two.

On occasion I'd steal a beer from the car or from the cooler, head off into the thick brush, gulp it down, and return to watch the rest of the game. I had to be fast about it because the brush doubled as the community urinal, and there was a lot of pissing going on back there. One evening while I was enjoying a Pabst Blue-Ribbon in the community piss-pot, I was surprised by one of my dads' teammates.

"Hey, Tommy; what do you know, buddy?" I quickly threw down the beer and unzipped my pants and pretended to urinate. "Oh, uh, nothing; just taking a piss." He stood with his back to me.

"Your dad's playing some good ball. Some good ball."

"This guy is pissing a six-pack," I thought. "Is he ever going to stop?"

Finally after a couple of grunts and a snort, he finished. "Well, got to get back to the ball game, Tommy. Say, does your dad know where you are?"

"Uh, no, but I'll be right there." Damn! A perfectly good beer gone to waste.

At one end of the ball field there was a boat ramp. The areas on either side of the baseball field were overgrown with brush and trees. They provided a perfect place for a kid to hide. That's where we built The Shack, roughly two hundred yards from the baseball diamond and unseen from the road.

Jake, Mitch, Ralphie, and I put it together with scraps of wood we found here and there. Others like Vern had provided additional labor, tools, and building materials. Vern appointed himself quality control inspector. I couldn't hammer a nail in straight to save my life, and Vern never failed to notice. We put in a wood-burning stove, some rickety chairs, and a car seat. We somehow managed to put shingles on the roof, but it still leaked here and there.

The Shack was our home away from home. It was a gathering point, a place to go when there was nowhere else to go. If you wanted to find a friend, the first place to look was The Shack. It was a butt-ugly structure, but it was our butt-ugly structure. On the other side of The Shack there was a small, manmade inlet that was good for fishing. I fished there all the time. I liked fishing; it was yet another form of escape for me, and I just liked being near the water. I would soon introduce a friend to The Shack and to that little, manmade bay.

It was a sunny summer afternoon, and I was visiting a friend—a female friend I had an interest in (and she in me). Her name was Roxanne. She had dark hair and an olive complexion. Roxanne was drop-dead gorgeous, and she liked me. She must want something from me, but what? "Why would she like me?" I used to ask myself. But she did. She really did. What did she want from me? It scared me to death.

Dear Tom,

You were a natural athlete. You could run like the wind, you had quick reflexes, and you had good hand-eye coordination. During the summer of 1969, or maybe it was 1970, you played baseball. The field was just a block or two from your grandparents' house where you lived with them and your dad. That was also the summer you took extraordinary interest in a member of the opposite sex. Her name was Roxanne. No kidding.

You had baseball practice that summer evening, but you would have preferred to go over to Roxanne's. Then you found an opening. Your Dad said he would be home late from work that day; he had some things to tend to. That was the opening. You decided you would skip out on baseball practice and head over to Roxanne's on your bike.

It was nice just to be around her. Scary too. She was an especially attractive girl. You thought, why in the world would someone like that take an interest in you? But she did. You would never pursue any kind of relationship with her though. First of all you were just fourteen, and second, you were too shy, too uncertain, too afraid. How does one exactly have a relationship anyway? How does it work? You thought it was maybe about heavy petting; that's all you could think of anyway. Sex equates with love.

Anyway the sight of Roxanne made your adrenaline rush and your heart get light. And after a bit you headed home. The path home took you across the baseball field. When you arrived your team was still practicing. Damn, this was not good. And, oh shit, there was your dad way over there. Jesus, were you in some deep trouble. You know what it meant.

Now your day quickly went from good to bad. You had an adrenaline rush; your mind went in a million different directions. How do I get out of this? After wasting some time aimlessly biking around, you went home. You had a plan. Get it over with quickly. So you walked into the house. Your dad was on the couch, and your grand parents were in their chairs. "Let's get this over with," you said to your dad. Without a word he got up from the couch, and followed you down to the basement.

"Lower your pants," he said. As you did, you could hear him remove his belt. And then he hit you with it.

So there you were, fourteen years old, and getting a beating with a belt. Just an hour or so ago you were on cloud nine, and now your dad was beating you. It was as if Roxanne were there watching. It was humiliating. You started to cry, not because it hurt so much—it did—but, hell, you could take that all day. Go ahead and hit me. You cried because your dad, this man who was a role model, someone you admired and someone you hated, was beating you with a belt.

Your insides were screaming, "I'm your son; why are you hitting your son? You don't do this to your son."

But he did. It wasn't the first time, and it wouldn't be the last. You hated this life.

You started to imagine a time when you would be an adult. Bigger than he was. You weren't going to take it anymore. "Revenge is a bitch, and I'm going to kick the living shit out of you, you motherfucker!" That's what you were thinking. In fact, later in life, maybe a year or two later when he was threatening you, you turned to him and said coldly. "Someday I'm going to be bigger than you, and someday will be here sooner than you think." It was a dare of sorts. He backed off. He understood the meaning; it was all over his face.

I know growing up in violence left its mark on you. You've dreamed about it on and off for years. When you were younger you dreamed of running away from your father as he chased you. As you grew older you dreamed of taking a stand and finally taking a swing.

Today he's an older man, a different man. But as you think of those years gone by, you think of a man who you simply hoped would vanish, and who you hoped would change.

You'll be all right. You were resilient then; you're resilient now. We'll talk again.

Take care my friend.

There was a flask of some sort of liquor in the dining room. I had noticed it the moment I walked in. "What's in there?" I asked, as if I didn't know it was alcohol.

"Oh, I think that's brandy." She evidently detected my interest. "You can have some if you want."

"Is that 'I dare'?" I asked.

"If you want it to be," she replied. I thought that there was no better way to impress a girl than to ply myself with alcohol, and I was very willing to do just that. A dare really wasn't necessary, though. All she had to do was ask. So, she brought out a glass, poured a drink and handed it to me. I gulped down the first glass, then another, then another. She would certainly be impressed with this. Now I was beginning to feel comfortable around her.

"Hey, let's see if anyone is down by The Shack," I proposed. So we left the house and started to make the long walk toward The Shack; but the world was starting to spin.

She held me by the arm. "Are you okay?"

"Oh yeah, I'm okay," I said.

"Let's take a bike. I'll drive. You get on the handlebars," suggested Roxanne. Who was I to argue? If she had suggested leaping off the roof of the house, I probably would have done it. So I somehow managed to get on the handlebars and off we rode. We zigzagged through neighborhood streets until we came to the main road in town. We had to cross it to get to The Shack; there was simply no other way.

The main road was busy on this day, and we couldn't find a spot to cross. We waited. It was warm, and the sun was beating down on us. I looked left, then right. Things were moving in slow motion. "Well, that's about enough. I'll get us across," I blurted.

"I don't think you should," Roxanne started to say, but I interrupted.

"Aw *fuck* that. I'm going to stop these fuckin' cars." So I did. I wobbled out into the street, found the center line, and slowed, if not completely stopped, traffic. Horns blared, and people cursed. Damn, I thought I was going to puke. Roxanne, on the other side of the road, was looking at me as if she were looking at someone who had gone insane. I waved her across.

"I can't believe you just did that," she said with her mouth agape.

"Really?" I said proudly.

"Yeah, really!" But I don't think she was impressed. We continued on our way down the gravel road, onto the path that took us through some brush and to The Shack.

"Where is everybody?" Then we heard voices over by the bay. I stumbled through some brush, and there they were; about a half-dozen friends. "Hey everybody," I blurted, "what's going on?" I asked with a shit-eating grin. It was apparent that I was drunk, but some just couldn't believe it.

"Is he really drunk? It's the middle of the afternoon."

"Yeah," Roxanne answered, "he's drunk." I was irritated that they had not asked me. Roxanne was not my mother, Goddamn it. "You want to know if I'm drunk, you ask me," I thought. So I lowered my pants and exposed my skinny rear end. "Hey, I got a big kiss for you."

Roxanne covered her eyes, "Oh my God." It didn't go over as well as I had hoped.

"What the hell!" I heard someone say. "Okay, let's throw him in—sober him up." I was ready for battle.

"You can fuckin' try, but I don't think any of you has the balls to do it." I was a gangly, skinny kid, and they were all bigger than I was, but I was scrappy.

Before they tossed me in the water I remembered I had my brand new leather cowboy boots on; very popular footwear at the time. "Hold it, *hold it.* Take my boots off first," I insisted.

"Okay, take his boots off."

"Hey, thanks a lot, man. Put them in The Shack."

"Okay, put them in The Shack," someone said. Then they tossed me in, and down I went, and I didn't come up. I just remember thinking that it wasn't that bad, not bad at all. The water was surprisingly warm, and it felt good. The next thing I remember is someone pulling me onshore, and screaming "Get him up, get him up!" I coughed and spit up water. The world was spinning around me. A face here, an arm there.

"You okay, Tommy? C'mon, man, you okay?" They carried me to The Shack, and they put me on a car seat that functioned as a couch. I promptly threw up, then again and again. I stayed on the "couch" the remainder of the day. My friends, at least some of them, stayed as well. They had a sense of the inner demons I was fighting. At least I believed they did. They knew my parents were divorcing. They knew that I drank a lot. Even some fourteen-year-old kids know when too much is too much. They sort of took it upon themselves to be my caretakers in a way, and I liked that.

Roxanne went home, still traumatized by my exposed butt-cheeks. She kept on trying to get to know me, to get close to me, but I never let her. I ran in the opposite direction. Around dinnertime I was feeling well enough to walk around. "See you tomorrow, Tommy?"

"Yeah," I said, "see you tomorrow." I continued with the dry heaves for another couple of hours, and then I went home.

CHAPTER 10

My mom's attorney was Robert "Big Bob" Kingston. He was a friend of the guy she had had an affair with, my eventual stepfather, who was also an attorney. Mom's attorney's name was Jack. At the time I hated him with a passion. As far as I and my brothers were concerned, he was a first-class prick who was responsible for everything that went wrong with my parents' marriage. He wasn't responsible, of course. The marriage had been gone long before he arrived. It was early in the morning, and I woke up to the sounds of people in the kitchen. I got up and observed from the living room what was happening.

It was Jack and some other glassy-eyed fellow. They were sitting at the dinner table, and they were obviously drunk. My mom, in an old tattered bathrobe, was making them something to eat. Jack liked his vodka, and he was having it in a tall glass with his scrambled eggs and bacon. Without any apparent warning, my mom walked into the living room and fell to the floor sobbing. To this day I have no idea why she did that. Jack got out of his chair, walked into the living room, and stood over my mother. "Sue, look, look; it's your son; your son!" he said, slurring his words. I guess he was talking about me. "Go to bed," my mom grunted from the floor without ever looking at me. I looked at Jack, looked at my mom, and went to bed. The other fellow just sat there at the table, gave me a quick glance, and helped himself to Jack's eggs.

My dad was a quiet drunk, quite the opposite of Jack, who was loud and obnoxious when drinking. When he was drunk the entire neighborhood literally heard about it. He's the guy you'd see wearing the lamp shade. My body language spoke volumes. "You don't like me very much do you, Tom?" he once asked me while gulping down his vodka and tonic. I sat stoically and didn't say a word.

A few seconds passed. He sipped his vodka again. "Okay then. Fine, just as long as we understand each other." Jack was involved in politics and Civil Rights when it was not very popular in some circles to support civil rights. At least not in the small, all-white town I lived in. He had actually met John Kennedy, and he had an autographed photo, which I thought was very cool. There were rumors that black kids would be bussed into our all-white school. Of course we were not going to tolerate any niggers in our school, and we made bold proclamations asserting just that.

Although my dad has changed his thinking considerably since attaining sobriety, in those drinking days things were different. When he was arguing with my mother, my dad at times informed her that she was dating a "nigger lover." "He's twice the man you are," my mom replied. The kind of exchange kids love their parents to have. It went downhill from there.

As kids we threw around the term and really didn't think much about it. Shit, my dad's friends were once discussing Joe Frazier and Mohammad Ali. "Ali is a nigger's nigger," one would say. "And Frazier is a white man's nigger," said another. I sat there taking all this in. Intuitively it didn't seem right, but these were adults; how could they be wrong? Calling someone a nigger was on par with calling someone an asshole as far as we were concerned. It didn't matter what color you were.

We couldn't possibly appreciate its ugly history, just as we didn't appreciate the ugly history of the swastika. In a word, we were ignorant. It wasn't associated with discrimination, the KKK, or anything else. Ugly. It was just a word. Then I learned that it wasn't "just a word."

We're at the dinner table, and my brothers and I tossed the term around a few times. Finally Jack had heard enough. Raising his voice, he said. "That word is an ugly word. It makes you sound like idiots, and I don't *ever* want to hear you use it again." We sat stunned. He continued, "What do you know about that word?" No answer. "Then allow me to educate you." We got our education, and I never did use that word again, ever.

"Ignorance and fear are at the root of all our problems," he would say. I learned a valuable lesson that day from a person I didn't particularly care for. When Jack was sober, he made it difficult not to like him.

Jack wore a suit and tie, and he drove a big Buick. Man, I thought, what the hell is with the suit and tie. My dad never wore a suit and tie. Jesus, this guy really bugged me. He must think he's a big shot. "Hey, Jim. I got your big shot right here," I said grabbing my crotch. Punches were thrown, but fortunately none landed. We probably wouldn't have noticed anyway. We were drunk.

Dear Tom,

When you were a kid you could run like the wind. You won every race you ran back then: short races, long races. You had a lot of practice.

It must have been a summer day back in 1969 or 1970. You were home, and your mom was home. Your brothers? You didn't know where they were. Your dad lived at the time with his parents on Oak Street. You lived on Poplar Ave about a mile away. A middle-class house in a middle-class neighborhood. Eleven-fourteen Poplar Avenue. SH-4746 was the phone number. It's funny how some things are indelibly etched in your memory.

Your mom was dating another man at the time, her boss actually. An attorney by the name of Jack who would one day be your stepfather. All you boys detested him. He was the reason your parents were divorcing, or so you thought. It's funny how kids think. Despite the fighting, the yelling, throwing various objects, etc., you wanted your parents to stay together. That's what kids want. This divorce tore a hole in your soul, on top of the one already there. Certainly they would not get a divorce. This would surely all go away someday. But it didn't.

Anyway, your mom of course never liked the fact that you showed outward disdain for Jack, and she didn't handle it very well either. There was the time one morning before school when you and your brother were at the kitchen table. You said something about Jack. You can't remember what exactly, but it wasn't what your mom wanted to hear. So with a holler she lifted her nightie (I guess that's what you call it) and exposed herself. Not that it mattered all that much. You could see right through the damn thing anyway.

She seemed to recognize that she had really screwed up, looked out the window to make sure no one had seen, and tried to compose herself. You looked at your brother, got up from the table, and went to school. A great way to start the day. You wondered if there were others in school who had had a similar morning. Now how exactly were you supposed to concentrate on school? When you came home she was there, met you outside, and suggested that you not tell your father. You didn't say much, maybe "fine" or "okay." That youthful spark had been extinguished, and at fourteen you were already tired of life.

So there you are back in the house on Poplar Avenue that summer day and the subject of Jack comes up. You say something; your mom says something. She's got a broom in her hand. About the time she decides to come at you with the broom, something inside you says "run." You bolt out the door with your mother in pursuit, broom in hand, running down the street in this nice, middle-class neighborhood. It isn't the first time this has happened.

Your mom of course can not keep up with you. She gives up. You keep running toward your dad's house on Oak Street. You think she will probably chase you in the car, so you keep one eye on the lookout while hiding behind trees and buildings. When you are sure the coast is clear, you bolt another 100 yards or so. You have to cross the baseball field to get to your dad's house, and it seems like a long way to go. Could she be waiting for you in the dugouts? You dash across the field. You're almost there.

You are out of breath as you make it to your dad's door. He is home. You sit at the kitchen table and pour out your emotions. There is a piece of paper on the table, and a pen. You make circles in scribbles, pressing harder and harder into the paper. Your dad gently takes them away.

You notice a police car pulling into the driveway. You run into the bathroom and lock the door. Your mom has reported you as a runaway. The police officer isn't going to take you away. He just needs to see you. So you open the door and stand there with your head down, no eye contact. The policemen leaves. Your mom calls your dad, and you can hear them talking. Later you go home, and your mom has calmed down.

You later learn that she had paid some neighbor kids to find you. You wonder how this could be. This whole thing makes you feel a little, well, disjointed and on guard, always looking over your shoulder.

"How and when does this all go away," you thought to yourself? You'd learn soon enough. The answer to "when?" is, "it doesn't." The answer to "how" would come in a bottle.

More on that later. For now, take care.

Jack had an announcement to make at dinner tonight, my mother told us. So he began, talking slowly, his words measured. "As you boys know, your mother and I have been dating for some time now. I love your mother very much, and we plan to marry soon."

I interrupted. "Pass the salt."

My younger brothers continued to shovel food into their mouths, sensing the tension in the air. There were a few seconds of silence. Jack fidgeted in his chair and exchanged glances with my mom. Darting eyes from everywhere; something was brewing.

"Let me continue my thought first." He cleared his throat. "Your mother and I plan to marry soon and…"

"I would like the salt please," I asked once again. More silence. More fidgeting.

"Does, uh, anyone have anything else he would like to say?" Jack was now clearly a bit irritated. My brothers kept eating as if it were their last meal. Perhaps they thought it might be.

"Yes, I do. For the last time, can someone pass me the Goddamned *salt?*" My mother nearly choked on her food.

"Go to your room; *right now.* Go to your room!"

"I will," I said, "just as soon as I get the damned salt."

Jack weighed in. "I think you should do as your mother asked."

"Hold on right there. You're not my dad, so you don't tell me what to do." My brothers kept eating as if none of this were going on.

"*Goddamn it,*" my mother said as she stood up and threw down her napkin. "Can't I have just a little happiness?" She stormed into her bedroom and slammed the door. Jack sat quietly, just staring at me. I stared back.

My youngest brother Mike looked at me and broke the silence. "Do you still want the salt?" I got up and left the house. Despair, that familiar feeling of hopelessness, enveloped me once more. That ever-present lump formed in my throat, and the chip on my shoulder got bigger. I wanted to run—somewhere, anywhere. Why were things like this? I ran for a long time, and I finally found my way to The Shack. When I got back, Jack was gone. I never did get any dinner—or any salt.

The following morning my brother and I were eating our cereal; Corn Pops I think. Mom walked into the kitchen wearing a nightie, a see-through nightie. There was nothing underneath. Since my dad had left, she had worn that see-through thing all the time. I wondered sometimes whether my mom was really a loose woman. I began to suspect that she was. My dad had accused her of being one; perhaps he was right. I couldn't think of a reason why she would wear that nightie around us. Is she completely oblivious to the fact that we can see through that thing? No one ever said a word about it though.

She wore a scowl on her face on this particular morning; I knew that face. She was obviously in a pissy mood, stemming from the events of last evening. She couldn't help saying something. Biting her words off she muttered, "*You are going to start talking to Jack in a pleasant tone. Do you understand me?*"

I didn't say anything. "And if you have a problem with that, tell it to *Jesus,*" she said, biting off each word. "Tell it to Jesus" was one of her favorites. She walked to the kitchen sink and back to the table, her voice rising. "I've had just about enough of you. Do you understand?"

I was getting angry. "No, I don't understand. We don't want him around." The next thing my mom did was totally unexpected and totally insane. She lifted her nightie, exposing herself as she let out a scream. She suddenly realized she was doing this in front of the bay window and quickly covered herself. She did a quick scan out the window. Had anyone seen? My brother and I looked at each other, not knowing what to make of the situation. We were stunned and embarrassed. On my way home from school that day, my mom met me in the driveway. "Let's just keep this morning between us, okay? I'd rather you didn't tell your father." "Sure, Mom. I won't say anything." The feeling in my gut was never going away.

Anyway, Robert, "Big Bob," was an intimidating guy with a big house and a big yard that needed big work. According to my mom, I was just the guy to earn a little money cleaning it up. I wasn't thrilled about the thought of mowing grass and pulling weeds during the summer. I had better things to do, like, well, like just screwing around, maybe doing a little fishing down by The Shack.

Big Bob walked out to meet me wearing a tee shirt and dress pants, with the belt undone and his zipper open. His hair was a greasy mess, and he had a drink in his hand. "Everything you need to bring this shitty yard to life can be found in the garage," said Big Bob. He opened the door to the garage. "You know how to use all this stuff, don't you?"

"Oh, yeah, sure."

"Well then, it's all yours. Let me know when you leave." With that "Big Bob" turned and headed for the house. There were the lawn mower, rakes, shovels, gloves, and—*holy crap*—a case of vodka. Is that really a case of vodka? I looked at the box. I looked back toward the house just in time to see Big Bob go inside. Was anyone looking? I opened the box and, damn, it was full. This was akin to finding a hundred dollar bill. "This could come in handy someday," I thought. "Someday soon."

CHAPTER 11

One of the last things my dad used to say to me before leaving the house on weekends was, "Don't get caught, and if you do, don't tell them your name."

"Okay, Dad, I won't." I have this mental image of getting arrested. I'm sitting in the back seat of the police car, handcuffed, when one of the officers leans in and asks me my name. "Well, officer, I can't tell you that."

The police officer looks puzzled. "Really? Why not?"

"Well, just before I left the house, my dad told me not to tell anyone my name if I got caught."

The police officer understands now. "Oh, okay. Never mind."

My dad thought he was being clever, but, Jesus! I wish he would come up with something original. I was the only person among my peers who didn't have a curfew. "I have to be home by 11:00 PM. What about you, Tommy. What time do you have to be home?"

"Uh, whenever. I don't know." This was very surprising to most of my friends, but it made me feel like a big shot. So, off I went, typically over to Mitch's house first. From there, either on foot or on bikes, we proceeded to Jake's house, and then we finally met up with Ralphie on the other side of town.

Ralphie Welles had a nickname, "Worm," apparently given to him by his mother because, as a baby, he had "crawled around on the floor like a little worm." The name stuck, but I just could not bring myself to call someone I had known since the third grade "Worm."

"Man," Ralphie said in exasperation, "I wish you would call me 'Worm'; why don't you just call me 'Worm'? Everybody else does."

"No way. I'm not calling you "Worm." You've always been Ralphie to me. Your name is Ralphie. To hell with the *Worm* crap."

"Well, I'm not answering unless you call me Worm." But he did. He was a couple inches shorter than I was, and he wore Buddy Holly–style glasses. He lived just two houses down from ours in a house that needed paint—several coats of paint. Inside it was always cluttered, with stuff everywhere. They were evidently in need of more storage space, or of a garage sale. And the floors, well, I always felt off balance because they were warped. Ralphie had an older brother Billy, an older sister Lynn, and a younger sister Betsy.

Ralphie's parents spoke with a slight drawl. It reminded me of someone I had once known from Tennessee. Ralphie's mother was a very religious and petite woman, who stayed home. She was older than most of the other women in the neighborhood, and she generally just kept to herself. His father was a very large man, standing over six feet, and weighing something in the neighborhood of two-hundred-fifty pounds. He was the proprietor of a gas station, Hank's North Side Texaco.

Billy was second in command. Ralphie worked there in the summer, pumping gas and sweeping floors. He looked up to his older brother. He was proud of Billy, and Billy was his mentor. My dad had sold his seventeen-foot Lyman outboard, a beautiful boat, to Billy because he could no longer afford to keep it. Billy and Ralphie were out at the lake one summer day with other members of their family. Ralphie was fishing from the dock as Billy was bringing the boat in. He waved as he approached. The outboard engine suddenly quit and the boat eventually came to a stop, dead in the water, roughly seventy-five yards from the dock.

Ralphie wasn't alarmed, and he just kept fishing. Billy went to the back of the boat and was working on the engine when it suddenly caught fire. It quickly spread to the back of the boat. Now Ralphie was alarmed. Billy made his way to the bow, but the fire was spreading rapidly. Why doesn't he grab a life-jacket or a seat cushion? There was an explosion, and the boat began to sink. Billy couldn't swim.

Watching from the dock, Ralphie was screaming in a panic for help. He jumped into the water and walked until it was up to his neck. He couldn't swim either. He watched as his brother screamed for someone to help him before he went under the water for the last time. He always blamed himself for his brother's death.

Lynn was just a year older than I, with long silky hair past her shoulders. She had average looks and an above average body. She used to baby-sit us when my mom and Jack went out for the evening. I really didn't mind that she "sat" for us; hell, I didn't want to watch my brothers, I had other plans. I never knew for sure, but I think my mom was aware of my "other plans."

As soon as my mom and Jack pulled out of the driveway, I raided the booze cabinet. My mom started marking the booze level in the bottles. On occasion she and Jack would go around the block and drive by the house to be sure we weren't doing things we shouldn't be doing. We just waited a few minutes longer. Soon afterward friends and acquaintances would arrive at the house, and a small party would ensue. People would come and go for a good part of the evening.

Lynn, our baby-sitter, was a bit on the loose side. Actually she was a lot on the loose side, and I often took advantage of that, particularly after a few drinks. Ralphie and she had had an incestuous relationship that had happened in their parents' bedroom, of all places. Maybe this was Ralphie's way of telling his father to fuck off. No one ever talked about the relationship he had had with his sister. I knew about it only because I was there.

Ralphie also had a half-brother that he had never met. He had never wanted to meet him. His dad had had an affair, something Ralphie discovered after Billy died. Billy's death left a huge chip on Ralphie's shoulder. Ralphie was the only one in the family to ever know about it. Hank had been on the phone with his mistress, who was asking for more money to support their child. Ralphie was on the other phone, and he overheard the entire conversation. Afterward Ralphie approached Hank and stood in front of him with his hands in his pockets. "I, uh, could use some money," he casually told his dad.

"Well, then, I guess you need to put in more hours at the station," replied Hank as he leaned back in his chair, his eyes never leaving the newspaper. Ralphie looked around anxiously. His anger was bubbling to the surface. "No, *Hank,* you don't understand…." But before he could finish his sentence, Hank bolted up from the chair, offended at being referred to as "Hank" by his son, and backhanded him across the face, sending Ralphie to the floor.

"You don't get smart with me!" But Ralphie, getting up from the floor, interrupted. "I heard your little phone conversation, *Hank.*" Hank went white, stood wide-eyed for a second or two, choking on his words, and then slowly slid into the chair. "What do you want from me?" he whispered.

Ralphie, looked at himself in a mirror, took a comb from his back pocket, and casually combed his hair; his hair was always in place. He had Hank by the balls, and he knew it. "Like I said," still looking in the mirror, "I need some fuckin' money so I can get the fuck outta here."

Hank, staring straight ahead, reached for his wallet, "How much is this going to cost me, Ralphie?" Ralphie snatched the wallet out of Hanks hands and took out a wad of cash. "How about all of it," he said, as he threw the wallet back at his father. Hank sat stunned and, as Ralphie turned to leave, he said, "Ralphie, you're going to keep your mouth shut about this now? I mean, your mom, she don't…"

"I know damned well she don't know, *Hank.* As long as I keep getting the money I need, she ain't gonna know," he said, as he held up the wad of bills. Ralphie always, and I mean always, had money. "And *Hank,* you don't you ever hit me again. Not ever again." The door slammed behind him.

Our mission was straightforward that evening, and for that matter on any other evening. Find some booze! Didn't matter what kind or what brand. Beer, wine, or liquor, who cared? We were at a school dance when Vern approached with some news. "If you put an aspirin in a Coke, you can get really drunk," he said.

"What?" I asked rhetorically.

"This is no shit. I read about it."

"Really? Well, then, let's try it," said Mitch.

This was intriguing. Imagine getting "drunk" on Coke and aspirin. I could legally buy that stuff. We thought outside the box. If one aspirin will give you a buzz, imagine what four or five will do? So we drank a couple of Cokes with some aspirin and waited. The only thing we got was an upset stomach and a case of the shits. Vern still insisted that that Coke and aspirin would indeed get you drunk. According to him this was an "indisputable, scientific fact."

So getting drunk was really more than a mission; it was a quest. We would do whatever it took. With beer in our hands, we were in our element. We were cool, big shots, and the kings of our domain. After I had had a beer, I had a sense of calm. This evening was no different. We were walking down the alley that went through the neighborhood. It was a particularly dark evening, and we could barely see our hands in front of our faces. That night we were not having any luck finding anything to drink. As we shuffled our way down the alley, kicking stones along the way, Mitch spoke up, frustrated. "This is bullshit; what are we going to do about some beer?"

"Does anyone know where Sammy is? Maybe he can get some from his parents' basement," said Jake. No one knew where Sammy, a mutual friend, was. He wasn't at The Shack. As we continued to walk toward an uneventful evening, we came upon the home where I had done some yard work. The light-bulb went off. "I know where we can get all the booze we want." We all came to a stop.

"Knock it off, Tommy," said Ralphie.

"Right there in that garage there's a case of vodka."

"What? Are you sure about that?" Mitch whispered with heightened interest. Now we were all whispering.

"Don't screw around with us, man. This is nothing to bullshit about," Jake said.

"Fuck you. I'm telling you there's a case of vodka just inside the door." We all looked toward the house.

"How do you know?" asked Mitch.

"Because I saw it. My mom knows the guy." There were a few lights on in the house, but none illuminating the garage.

"I'm telling you, I saw it with my own eyes. It's in there." There we were, standing in a dark alley, hands in our pockets, gazing at the garage as if it were a holy place and vodka our god.

Finally Ralphie whispered, "Who's going to go get it." Before anyone else could volunteer, Mitch, not surprisingly, did.

Mitch Greene was small in stature, maybe a hundred pounds or so soaking wet. He had large, bulging eyes. "Helps me see better at night," he'd insist. He had just a tuft of hair in front that passed for bangs. He used his mom's Dippity-Doo to keep his hair in place, combed straight down and then across, just above the eyebrows. He lived just a short distance from my grandparents home.

His home, like Ralphie's, was in desperate need of paint, and the yard was usually overgrown with weeds. He had once had a German Shepherd that he had beat the shit out of for no particular reason as a puppy. The dog, as you would expect, became quite mean, and it bit me on more than one occasion. Mitch never believed it though. "Mitch, your damn dog just bit me!"

"Nah, he wouldn't hurt anyone."

"What do you mean? I'm telling you that your damned dog just bit me."

"And I'm telling you, he wouldn't hurt anyone." The dog finally attacked a little kid. The kid survived; the dog didn't. The dog was taken away and never heard from again. The neighborhood let lose with a collective sigh of relief. Mitch would never admit that the dog was nasty. "That dog wouldn't hurt a fly," he'd say.

Mitch sometimes seemed as if he had something to prove to us. I suppose he had something to prove to himself as well. Despite his small size he could scrap with the best of them. He reveled as I did in getting attention doing things no one else in his right mind would try. He picked fights with kids twice his size, and he got his ass kicked thoroughly, but he never seemed to mind too much—and he never backed down.

The other kid would usually tire from hitting Mitch and simply quit. Mitch, often with a bloody face, shouted insults after the guy, daring him to come back. He wouldn't, and Mitch would declare victory. Coming up with unflattering nicknames was really his forte. He came up with a beauty for our gym teacher, "Weasel." The name was fitting. The teacher did in fact *look* like a weasel. "My name is Mr. Banks!"

"Yes, Mr. Weasel, ah, I mean Mr. Banks."

"Okay, Greene, take an E." Weasel gave out E's like grandparents handed out candy. If we didn't get dressed for gym class we would "take an E." Swear in class, "Take an E." We took more than our fair share of E's.

Each of us was assigned a number, and we shouted it out as we counted off before each class. My number was twenty. As we lined up at the start of gym class, Mitch suggested that, when it came my turn, I should say "Twent-easel. I dare ya to say it."

"No, I'm not gonna say twent-easel," I said.

"What? You're not chicken-shit are you?"

"Fuck you." So the count-off began, "seventeen, eighteen, nineteen." Then came my turn, and I was not about to let Mitch get away with the chicken-shit comment. "*Twent-easel.*" The counting stopped there. There was dead silence. Twenty-one didn't happen. Everyone leaned over to see who in the hell had either the big balls or the small brain. Mr. Banks, with his whistle around his neck and clipboard in hand approached me, put his finger in my chest and said "Carter, my name is Mr. Banks. Take an E. Get dressed, and get the hell out of here."

Well, I couldn't have all the attention, so Mitch piped up, "Ah, I need to take a leak, Mr. Weasel, I mean, Mr. Banks."

"*Damn it!* Take an E. Greene, you get out of here too." So, Mitch and I got out of our smelly gym clothes (which were washed maybe once per month) and, instead of going to the principal's office, we took an early lunch.

A substitute teacher was easy pickings and something Mitch lived for. He was the predator; the substitute was his prey. Mitch would raise his hand. "Yes, Mitchell? You have a question?"

"Uh, yeah. I was just wondering whether you could explain menstruation." The substitute turned bright red, beads of sweat forming on her forehead; she stumbled through the answer. Mitch raised his hand again.

"Does anyone else have a question?" the substitute asked, looking about the room in vain for another question. "Yes, Mitchell, and this will be the last question."

"Uh, sure. What are tampons for anyway?"

"Okay, people, now we're going to watch a movie." That was Mitch. He wasn't shy about using four-letter words, and their use often provided him with some shock value. I supposed that had its purpose. He lived with his mother and older sister. Both frequently had guys over in their respective bedrooms, with doors shut. But anyone with a pair of ears knew what was going on in there.

His father's whereabouts were unknown. His mom didn't bother to find out. I suppose she really didn't care. He had gone to the bar just a couple of years previous, and he had never come back. No note, no nothing, just gone. Mitch rarely spoke of his father. "Where did your dad go?" I asked once.

"How should I know where that asshole is?" he'd say. I got the message. Mitch liked to drink for perhaps the same reason I did and, tonight he was prepared to do what was necessary. "I'll get it. Where is it again?"

"Just on the other side of the door, on the right-hand side," I instructed.

"The right-hand side? What right-hand side are you talking about?" he asked.

I was getting a little anxious. "When you open the stinking door, it will be on the floor just to your right, numb nuts." My dad liked to use "numb nuts," and I thought it was more a term of endearment than insulting; Mitch understood that. "Okay. I think I got it." We all stood anxiously in the alley as Mitch went over the split level fence and around to the front of the garage where he found the door. He ducked inside and closed the door behind him. "Why the hell did he close the door?" I asked no one in particular.

The door to the garage faced the house, and without warning a porch light came on. We did a collective "Oh shit" under our breath, and then we took a few steps back making sure we were still under the cover of darkness. A few minutes passed. No one came out. "What's that idiot doing in there?" Ralphie wondered.

"He's probably waiting for the lights to go out," I said. "Oh right. That makes sense." Ralphie was not one those brainiac types; the only books he ever read were pornographic. Not that there was anything wrong with that. Is there a fourteen-year-old kid that wouldn't go bonkers over a pornographic magazine?

"I know they're here someplace," Ralphie hollered as the rest of us waited in The Shack. "Okay, I got em!" Ralphie dug up the Playboy magazines and brought them into The Shack. There must have been at least a dozen Playboy magazines in the box we had buried them in. We each took one and sat around The Shack with our eyeballs bulging from their sockets, each lost in his own fantasy.

"I can see pubic hair on this one," said Ralphie. We all dropped what we were doing and dashed over for a look. We looked closely, and then Mitch spoke. "I don't see any pubic hair." His tone was one of disappointment.

"I don't either," I said.

"Look, hold it up to the light, and you can see it."

Jake took it and held it up. He handed it back. "I don't see it either."

"Well fuck you, then; I can," said Ralphie.

"Maybe in your dreams," said Mitch.

After a few minutes Ralphie got up from the car seat. "I've got a take a piss." He walked out of The Shack with Playboy in hand to "take a piss."

We looked at each other. Ralphie was known to choke the chicken anytime, anywhere. "Fuckin-A," cracked Jake, shaking his head. Mitch hollered after him, "No sticky pages, okay, Worm?"

Ralphie shot back. "Ah fuck you guys!"

We waited in the alley for what seemed like a long time, when in reality it was probably just a couple of minutes. Apparently Mitch had become impatient and decided to make a break for it. We watched as the door opened very slowly, and then out dashed Mitch holding a case of booze in his arms, bottles clanking; holding it as if it were a baby. "Here he comes!"

As he made the fence, we heard someone shout from the direction of the house, "Hey! Hold it right there!"

"Holy crap, run," I said. We took off running down the alley, and we could hear Mitch behind us having his share of problems running with a full case of vodka. "Goddamn it, *stop* you motherfuckers and help me!" We quickly took three to four bottles each and stuffed them in our jackets.

"C'mon, man," Mitch said. "He saw me. Let's get outta here." We crammed the cardboard case in a garbage can that had been left in the alley, and we continued running west. I thought that perhaps we were in the clear. Maybe Big Bob wasn't up for chase. We had made it about two, maybe three blocks, just catching our breath, when we saw the distant headlights of a car pull into the alley behind us. They were heading our way. We were perhaps twenty yards or so from a huge mulberry tree in which we had started to build a "club-house" of sorts. What we had done was basically put some plywood down; it was a place where we could sit, and that was about the extent of it.

"The mulberry tree; let's go!" Jake said.

Jake Sellers was a gangly kid with curly hair, a huge grin, big lips, and a mouth full of teeth. He had two sisters; one older and one younger. His mother stayed at home while his father drove a truck around the country. His father had been very disillusioned with his lot in life. He didn't particularly like traveling around the country, and he was deep in debt. He was found at a rest stop in Indiana. He had put a pistol in his mouth and pulled the trigger.

Jake never referred to him as his dad, but rather as "that gutless fucker." Jake was a bit uncoordinated, and he had never played sports, but he wished he could. He knew he couldn't play very well, "So why bother?" he'd ask people. He often hung out around baseball practice, smoking a cigarette, just standing there and watching. Once after baseball practice he grabbed me by the arm. "You up for doing something?"

"What do you want to do?"

Jake, like the rest of us, always enjoyed a good adrenaline rush. "Sammy's parents have some beer in a refrigerator." I looked at him, puzzled why he would be stating the obvious. They always had beer in the basement refrigerator. He could see that I was not quite getting it. "The basement, man; there's a window we can crawl through."

Now I was intrigued but cautious. "You're crazy; I'm not crawling through any damned window. Besides, what if we get caught?"

"Don't be a pussy; we're not going to get caught, man," he said as he took a drag from his cigarette. He sensed my hesitation. "Okay, I'll do it; you just sit on your ass and keep a lookout."

Sammy Perkins was a gentle giant and a mutual friend who lived in one of the wealthier parts of town. His dad was a very successful dentist. "You've got your drugs," he'd say referring to marijuana, "and we've got ours," he'd continue, holding up a glass of whiskey. By the time we got to Sammy's house, it was getting on toward dusk. We went to the window. There were Sammy's mom and dad reading the paper, watching television, and drinking their whiskey. It was looking good. We went to the basement window. The room was lit, and there was the old refrigerator. But the window was too narrow, and the drop to the floor was too high.

"No way can you get in there," I said.

Jake thought for a second. "You stay here. I'll be right back."

"Hey wait. Where are you going?" I whispered. Jake ran to the back door, and I waited. "Shit!" I whispered to myself. I was getting anxious. I looked toward the basement window, and for the love of Jesus, there was Jake. He waved at me with his big grin. I waved back, not quite believing what I was seeing. He opened the refrigerator, grabbed a six pack, reached up to the window, and handed it to me. "Here. I'm going to get one more." He had simply sneaked into the house. No one had noticed. We got the adrenaline rush and, more important, twelve beers. We drank around three to four apiece, and we buried the rest down by The Shack.

So here we were, running in the alley after the vodka heist, looking for some place to hide. We ran to the mulberry tree, and then it occurred to me that we were still carrying the booze; our arms were not exactly "free." "I can't climb any tree. How am I supposed to get up the damn tree with these bottles in my arms?" I asked in a moment of sheer brilliance.

We quickly looked around for a place to stash the bottles as the headlights closed in. "There," said Ralphie, "stash them in the bushes." So, we stashed our booty in the bushes and scurried up the tree and onto the platform. The tree was old and very large. It had many dead branches, and the plywood we had tacked down a couple of years earlier was a bit warped. So, the four of us sat quietly while the car approached. We could clearly see a beam from a flashlight coming from the car. If we were spotted, we were dead meat. The car was perhaps seventy-five yards away. A branch made an unpleasant cracking noise. No, this was not happening, I thought.

"Are we safe here?" Ralphie whispered. "I don't think so," I whispered back.

"Fuckin-A," said Jake.

"Maybe we should all hold on to another branch," I suggested. The car passed slowly underneath us and then stopped. It was no flashlight coming from the car, but rather an attached spotlight. The markings were obvious. "It's the cops," Jake whispered.

"Oh shit," Mitch responded. No one was breathing. There were more cracking noises from the tree. "What the fuck is he doing?" Mitch asked.

"Everybody, just be quiet." I whispered slowly. Then, more cracking noises. The car started moving again, and, as we let out a collective sigh of relief, the branch gave way. Everyone except for Mitch had taken my advice and latched on to another branch. The branch, the plywood, and Mitch all fell to the ground, maybe fifteen feet or so. By the grace of God, the police car kept moving. We climbed down to find Mitch alive, but with scrapes on his hands, and a nasty cut on his leg just below the knee, bleeding badly.

After cutting loose with a few choice four-letter words, a hobby of sorts, Mitch reminded us of our mission. "Let's get the booze and get down to The Shack now," he said. The guy had his priorities. Jake had gone directly to the bushes to retrieve the treasure, ignoring the injuries his friend had sustained. The rest followed. As Mitch limped along we finally made it to safe haven—The Shack. In the distance we could see the lightening flashes of an approaching storm.

"Where are we going to hide this stuff?" asked Jake.

"Yeah, I'm not sharing this with anyone; I can tell you that right now," I said. "We earned it."

"Damn straight, we're not sharing this with anybody," said Ralphie. "If Vern hears about this, everyone in town will find out about it, so whatever you do, don't tell Vernon."

This was ours. We had worked hard for it, and we had risked our asses for it. It was like gold, and no one would share in it. So we looked for a place to hide the vodka, and we finally found a soft sandy place to bury it. The sand was the texture of flour, so we could easily dig the hole ourselves. "Easy does it. Don't break 'em." All the bottles went carefully in the hole except for one. With that one we celebrated our adventure and our prize, and soon Mitch felt no pain whatsoever in his leg.

Then there was a flash, a clap of thunder, followed by the inescapable downpour. Everyone ran inside The Shack. Well, almost everyone. I stayed in the rain, but it wasn't long before the guys ran outside, grabbed my arms, and carried me inside.

About ten years later, in an ironic twist of fate, Big Bob represented my wife in our divorce. He was a real prick, but that was his job; he was a divorce attorney. I walked away with nothing but my clothes. Perhaps that is what is meant by poetic justice. But on that dark, stormy summer night, we got the vodka.

CHAPTER 12

Marty Williams was Vern's older brother by three years. Later in life he would become the chief of police for the same small town we all grew up in. Some of the guys he hung out with could be the bullying type, but Marty really seemed to be a genuinely nice guy, and he helped me out of some tough spots.

The city water tower sat on the school property. Today, there is a fence around the tower to keep would-be climbers away, but at that time there was no fence. One could actually climb all the way to the top, but no one ever seriously thought about doing it, or at least no one we knew. That night the four us had been drinking and discussing what to do as we walked near the tower. Underneath the tower we noticed something going on. "Let's check it out," said Ralphie. A group of friends and acquaintances had congregated in the area, smoking, having a beer, and just bullshitting. We joined them.

Jake and I both looked upward. "How high do you think that sucker is?" asked Jake.

"I don't know," I answered. "Maybe we should find out."

"What?" Jake asked, chuckling under his breath. We both just stared straight up; there was a red collision light blinking on and off at the very top, which reminded me of a blinking eye.

"I'm going up," I said.

"Fuckin-A you are." Jake said, making it sound more like a question than anything else. So I started up, in no condition to climb steps, let alone climb a tower ladder. No one noticed that I was climbing until Jake shared the exciting news.

Mitch walked over next to Jake. "Who's that?"

"Tommy's climbing the tower." Everyone turned to look, and that's the whole purpose of pulling a stunt like this. I was getting noticed. Sheer adrenaline. *Damn,* I was important, I thought.

"Tommy, don't do that, man," someone said. "You can get arrested for that; come on man; come back down."

Ralphie was more to the point. "Tommy, what the hell are you doing? Get your ass down here before you fall and kill yourself." But I kept on. "Okay, asshole, go ahead and kill yourself, I don't give a shit."

My mother has been in the bathroom for a long time. She ran in there in tears after I had told her I disapproved of Jack. What in the hell was she doing in there? I paced back and forth with my stomach in knots. Why does she do this shit? "Mom, what are you doing in there?" No response. "Mom, c'mon, what's going on in there?"

"Nothing," she said. "Go away."

"Mom, are you hurting yourself? You're not hurting yourself are you?" A pause. "Maybe. Maybe I am," she sobbed. "Maybe I am."

God, what am I supposed to do about this? Why do I have to do anything about this? Is she cutting her wrists, taking some pills?

"Mom!" I was now pleading. "You've got to come out. Listen, Mom, I like Jack. I like Jack, okay? Please come out!" A few seconds passed. The door opened, and my mom walked out—and I wanted to scream.

"Can you hear me? Go ahead then. Go ahead and kill yourself, man." That was just the way Ralphie talked to his friends. It was the way we talked to each other. It was endearing in a way that only we understood. The attention I was getting was exhilarating. I couldn't stop now. The thought of failure kept driving me all the way to top. I had made it, and I was feeling a bit light-headed.

I looked down. "Come on up, you cowards," I said, laughing. No one took me up on the offer; I was not sure whether anyone even heard me. I sat down with my back against the tower. I looked skyward, and I remember that I noticed how many stars there were. I was consumed by them, and remember thinking that there must be a God. Only a God could do that, I thought. How could there not be a God? I hope there's a God. Life at that moment could not have been any better. There were so many stars; it was hard to take my eyes off them.

"Right there is the Big Dipper," my dad said, pointing to the sky.

"Oh yeah," I responded, "I can see it!"

My dad and I were sitting on the picnic table, stargazing in the backyard.

"Can I have another sip?" I asked.

"Sure," my dad said as he handed me the beer. *"But don't let your mom smell that on your breath."*

"Okay," I said taking a sip. *"What's that?"* I asked as a small light passed in the sky.

My dad looked at it for a second. *"That looks like a satellite."*

"Cool. What's it for?" I asked.

"I really don't know; could be a lot of things."

"I really like looking at the stars, Dad."

"Yeah, me too; makes you feel kind of small, doesn't it?" my dad answered.

"You know what I want to be when I grow up?" I asked, taking another sip of beer.

"What's that?"

"I think I'd like to be an astronaut."

"You can be anything you want," he said.

"Yeah," I said, *"I want to be up there with the stars."*

"Hey, Tommy," someone shouted. "Get your ass down here; we're taking off." I didn't want to leave, but somehow I made it to the ground, and Jake rewarded my efforts with another beer.

"You're insane, man; you're insane." I chugged the beer and started feeling the effects of several beers, and I was having some difficulty walking. I was also getting loud, and I started singing Led Zeppelin's "Dazed and Confused." *"I've been dazed and confused for so long…."* I tripped and fell to the ground, cutting my bottom lip. It bled down my chin.

"We gotta get him home and in bed," Ralphie said.

As my friends helped me walk across the school property and out the gate, Marty pulled up in his car. "What's going on guys?"

"Tommy's drunk again. He needs to go home."

Marty thought for a second and then said, "Put him in the car; I'll take him home." And so he did.

"Tommy, Jesus, what happened to your lip, man?" he asked on the drive home. I didn't answer; perhaps I couldn't. Things were going black, and I passed out in the back seat. He carried me past Ralphie's sister Lynn and into my room where he took my shoes, socks, and pants off and put me in bed. He didn't have to do that. He cared. That's how I took it anyway, and I never forgot it.

Dear Tom,

You remember the night many years ago when you stayed at your great-grand-parents' house? That creaky, old, drafty home across the lake and in a of part town that was not especially good? You were maybe ten or eleven. Gram and Trip. You don't recall why in the world your great-grandfather was referred to as Trip, but there you have it.

He had a deep, firm, strong voice that got your attention real quick. He was a strong man, and I don't necessarily mean physically strong. You trusted him; he had a presence about him. People respected him. He was also a very gentle and kind man. He and your great-grandmother loved each other very much, and they had no trouble showing their affection for one another.

Affection was a rare sight in your home. You recall the time Trip came back from the hospital; he had lost consciousness for reasons you are unsure of and had fallen to the floor. It was a struggle for Gram to get to the phone, but she did. He had been at the hospital for a few days, and now he was coming home. Gram could hardly wait to see him. You were sitting near Gram when he was being helped through the backdoor and into the house. Gram turned and looked over her shoulder expectantly

She called him by his name. "Frank," she called, "Frank, is that you?" She kept trying to twist in her chair so she could get a better look as he came through the kitchen doorway. As he literally shuffled his way toward her, he passed you and gave you a reassuring wink. Then Gram reached out with her arms. "Frank. Are you all right?" He bent down without saying a word, and he gave her a kiss. Poetry. There were a lot of years together between the two of them. Camping together, fishing together, hunting together, and now just being together.

As for their grandchildren, well, you could tell by the sparkle in Gram's eyes that she thought her grandkids and great-grandkids were just about the most precious things on the planet. Gram had a broken hip that hadn't healed quite right. So she spent almost all of time in her chair with her leg propped up on a pillow. Her foot always seemed badly swollen and bruised, and she used a walker to get around as best she could.

You used to eat Thanksgiving dinner at their home, and do you remember what was served? Yup. Kentucky Fried Chicken for Thanksgiving, and it was just about the best meal you had ever had. Gram always used to say, "Eat slow now, and eat a lot. She would say it at least two dozen times. Your Uncle Budd and Aunt Evelyn were there as well. Your aunt (actually your dad's aunt) was your grand-mother's sister. She adored you, and she had a habit of giving you big, wet kisses. That was all right. In your heart of hearts, it made you feel good.

There was one day, one winter's day I believe, when your dad turned to you and said he wanted to tell you something, but it shouldn't be repeated. He said ol' Trip had been more of a father to him than your grandfather had been. For some reason that didn't come as a compete surprise. Your grandfather could be a real SOB. Trip had taught your dad how to hunt, fish, and camp, and I do believe Trip did his level best to teach him how to be a father. You sometimes wish that they had spent more time together.

Well, first Gram died, and it was tough to see Trip so broken up over it. He said to you after her funeral, "I want you to remember her the way she looked today." Her hair was made up, of course, and she had on some jewelry, and she wore a blue dress. He wanted you to remember her in the blue dress. Trip thought she was beautiful. And she was. In many ways she was more beautiful than words can describe.

Your mom took you and your brothers over to Trip's house after the funeral. She was as naturally emotional as was Trip. She had something to say to Trip. She was choked up, but she managed to get out an apology. Trip suggested that there was really no need for that. But she asked Trip to forgive her for the past. She was talking about the divorce that your parents had just gone through. And you know what? Trip forgave her in an instant, just like that. As I said before, everyone respected him, and it was important for your mom that he forgive her. They hugged, and it was over. You bit down on a pencil so you wouldn't cry; in fact you bit down so hard you broke it. At the time it was a gut-wrenching thing, but as you look back, that was truly one of life's bitter-sweet moments. There is something quite natural and quite beautiful about it.

Trip died about a year or two later, and it was tough on your dad. He really loved that guy, and so did you.

Now you're back on the couch over at their home watching their black and white TV set. You're covered up with a blanket, and you're getting sick to your stomach. You've got a little virus. You vomit just a bit on the floor. You tense up as if you had done something wrong. Jesus, if Dad finds out you threw up on the floor…But Gram gives a reassuring look. It's okay. You didn't do anything wrong. You're a little boy, and you're sick, and we're here to take care of you. And look, here comes Trip and he's not mad at all. Why, you don't have to get up and run to the bathroom. He's bringing you a pan. He's actually bringing you a pan so you don't have to get up. And you can tell he's concerned. He tells you to lie back down. It's going to be all right.

He was a giant. They both were.

Take care, my friend.

CHAPTER 13

Marty pulled up along the curb in his parents' Plymouth Fury with a couple of other guys we knew. Mitch and I were walking toward Jake's house. "Hey guys!"

"Hey, Marty, what's going on?" He looked down at the steering wheel, looked straight ahead.

"We, uh, we heard that you guys have some vodka."

His buddy next to him pressed the issue. "You guys can't *possibly* drink all that vodka!" he was almost shouting. *Son of a bitch,* someone had told Vern. We were caught off guard, yet we felt like big shots at the same time. We were smart-assed sophomores; these guys were seniors, and we had a whole case of vodka!

"Yeah," I said looking around, "I guess we got some."

"Where did you guys get a case of vodka anyway?" he asked.

Mitch shrugged his shoulders and said matter-of-factly, "We stole it."

"Yeah, well," Marty started, "why don't you just give us a few bottles? I mean you guys aren't going to drink all of it, right?" I hesitated, my eyes darting around as if someone might overhear us.

"How many bottles are we talking about?" I asked.

"How about three? Give us three bottles."

The guy next to him shouted "No way, Marty; they give us *half.*"

"Fuck you!" Mitch said, "We stole it, it's ours."

"You watch your mouth, Greene or I'll kick your scrawny little ass."

"You can try, asshole," Mitch shot back.

Marty threw up his hands. "Hold it. Just hold it! Three bottles, just three, and we'll give you a ride to your party. That okay with you, Tommy?"

I looked at Mitch. He shrugged his shoulders. What were we going to do? "Yeah, okay. Meet you down at The Shack in about an hour or so."

The four of us sat around The Shack waiting for Marty. "I don't get it. How did Vernon find out about the vodka?" I asked to no one in particular.

"Fuck if I know. I haven't even seen the guy lately." Mitch said.

"Well, someone told him."

As we debated on who the snitch was, Marty pulled up in his car and made his way to The Shack. "Hi guys. What did you do with the booze, bury it?"

"Yeah." We looked at each other. "How did you know?"

"Shit," he said with a light laugh, "you guys bury everything." *Goddamn* that Vernon! We dug up our booty in the soft sand as Mitch complained about giving some of it away.

"Jesus, Mitch, we've got eight bottles left. How much do you need?"

"It's the principle of the thing. *We* stole it."

That was logical, and it made perfect sense to me. Anyway we gave them their three bottles, and all four of us crammed in the back seat of his car, holding our precious cargo under our coats. The guy in the passenger seat lit his cigarette and turned to the back. "Are you really planning to drink all of that?"

We looked at each other a bit puzzled by the question.

"That's a lot of booze, you know." He turned to face the windshield. "Damn, if I drank that much booze," he said taking another drag from his cigarette, "I'd kill myself."

"We can handle the booze," Mitch said.

"Uh-huh," he said taking another drag. "Sure you can."

We arrived and got out of the car with the bottles clanking under our coats. I started heading for the party when Marty called out, "Tommy, come here a sec."

I ran back to the car. "Yeah, what is it?"

Marty paused for second. "Listen, just be careful tonight. You know, just take it easy."

"Yeah, sure; no problem," I replied. "If you need a ride home, call me."

Marty wrote down his phone number and handed it to me. "Thanks Marty." I said. "I'll do that."

Dear Tom,

It's sad to see you depressed. You weren't when you woke up this morning. But then you started thinking of the past. I wonder why, particularly when it upsets you so. Nothing you can do about it now anyway, is there?

You're fourteen years old; your best friend is over to the house. Your mom and dad are arguing in the kitchen. Your mother has a "legal secretaries meeting" to go to, but you and your dad know different. She's having an affair; screwing some guy down at the office. But the words are never spoken. Maybe if it's not said, it's not true. Maybe it goes away. Your dad won't give her the car keys. Your mom quite suddenly goes for the drawer, pulls out a knife, and threatens your dad with it, all in front of you and your friend.

Remember when she did the same to you? You left the house in spite of what she told you. You came back quite late with beer on your breath. And quite suddenly she went for the kitchen drawer and pulled out a knife and held it to your throat. You could feel the point of the knife, and you were afraid to blink. She finally put the knife away. You started to walk upstairs, stopped, and turned to say something. You were steaming mad. "You are nuts. Fucking nuts!"

Anyway your dad took the keys and threw them behind the refrigerator; your mom got them anyway, and she left. Your dad sloshed down another bottle of Blatz. A case was in the garage; and it would be gone before she got back.

The next morning your dad stormed into the kitchen with condoms in hand, "Why the hell are these things in your purse?" You were not supposed to understand the meaning, but you did.

You don't remember what happened after that, but it was par for the course around your house, wasn't it? Fighting, hollering like you kids were not even there. But you found peace and security in the attic. Way back in the attic. Nobody went back there. Oh, they could if they wanted, but no one ever did. You imagined putting up a false wall and simply living back there. It was safe.

I'm angry about this, though. Goddamn, what was wrong with these people? Did they know that the fighting, arguing, and name calling tore a hole in your guts? It's little wonder you would have your first blackout in just a few short months. Getting drunk was a way to escape. Whoever invented booze should get a medal, right? Feeling numb was better than feeling angry, anxious, and sad. "Happiness, well, that's fleeting, and only fools believe in that," you thought.

I know how you feel. You feel these people, your parents, stole your childhood. They had an obligation to protect you. They didn't, and they didn't seem to care. "They're a couple of dumb-asses," you'd tell your friends. You loved them, and you hated them.

Sometimes you wonder what the big deal is. I know. You think, "Christ, this happened 30-some years ago," right? Well then why does it feel like it happened yesterday? You can't push this under the rug and pretend it doesn't exist. And you can't drink it away either. Been there, done that, right?

Listen, you have my permission to be happy from this point forward, at least for today. We'll talk more later.

Take care, my friend.

CHAPTER 14

The path to the party was through the garage and down the stairs. The room was dimly lit, and the smell of sickly sweet incense filled the air. Jimi Hendrix was playing on the cheap record player where people were huddled looking over album jackets. It seemed like it was always Hendrix or Led Zeppelin. We were particularly fond of "The Lemon Song" simply because the lyrics suggested sex. Late at night after a few beers we walked down the street singing "The Lemon Song". Evidently it was not the favorite of everyone. A porch light came on here and there, and it was not long before we saw the police cruiser.

After we had ditched our beer, the cruiser put the spotlight on us. "You guys making all the noise out here?"

"No, sir," I said, pointing in another direction, "it's coming from over there." The officer took a look in the direction and then looked at me. "Uh-huh. Just keep it down. You shouldn't be walking around the streets this late anyway."

The officer gave me another look. "Aren't you Tommy Carter, Frank Carter's kid?" I had a flashback to my dad telling me not to tell 'em my name if I got caught. "Yeah, I guess so." In this small town the police knew who we were and who our parents were, so it was not a huge surprise when my dad asked me later about my singing prowess.

At the party groups of people congregated in their usual cliques. There were some on the floor, some on the couch, and some just standing around. I was amazed at how much alcohol there was. Beer, cheap wine, liquor, and plenty of it. In retrospect I guess it just *seems* amazing. At the time all was the way it was supposed to be. The hosts' parents were in the kitchen having dinner with some friends; one of whom just happened to be our science teacher. As we entered the home, Mitch noticed Mr. Blackmore, and the temptation to say *something* was just too much for him.

"Hello, Mr. Blackmore."

"Oh, hello, Mitchell."

"Are you still teaching sex ed, Mr. Blackmore?"

"Yes, Mitchell, I'm still teaching sex ed."

"Oh, that's great. Well, nice talking to you, enjoy your dinner."

"Thanks, Mitchell. Always a pleasure."

"Pleasure is all mine, Mr. Blackmore." The guy was tenacious. People kept coming in the door and continued down the stairs. And so did the four of us, with our arms wrapped around our coats, ensuring that the vodka didn't fall to the floor. It had to be obvious, but we thought we were pulling off something clever. After a few swigs of the vodka, I had some cheap wine, followed by some beer and more cheap wine. All I had to do was ask. How much beer, wine and vodka, I haven't a clue, but it was enough to boost my confidence. I just didn't know when enough was enough.

My ability to socialize had become easy. I became friendlier with members of the opposite sex. Girls I would never dream of approaching were now easy to talk to. The only way I would ever approach these girls was if I were plastered with alcohol. Tonight was one of those nights. Some brushed me off; others didn't. It didn't bother me though. I bumped into people and into walls. I fell over things on the floor. The combination of the smell of cheap wine and the burning incense was sickening, as Hendrix continued to play in the background. "Don't they ever play anything else?" I thought.

"How about some Led Zeppelin," I blurted out. No one paid any attention to my request. "I said, how about some Goddamned *Led Zeppelin!*"

Ralphie grabbed my shoulder, "Jesus, Tommy, calm down, man. Here, have a beer."

"Yeah, a beer. Okay, I'll have a beer. Long live Jimi Hendrix!"

Eventually I ended up on the floor with a girl. My head was in her lap, and she pulled her fingers through my hair. It was a small slice of heaven. Then the room began to spin; talk about lousy timing. I sat upright, feeling sick to my stomach, and then I bolted up the stairs. I threw up next to a car in the garage, and then I walked around to the side of the house where I sat down in the cool grass. I just needed a little fresh air; I was already feeling better, but then I passed out.

"*Tommy, Tommy*, get up, man; time to get up." It was Mitch shaking me awake. "C'mon back and party. What the hell are you doing out here, man?" he asked.

"Okay, I'll be there in a minute." But I never made it back to the party. The party had ended early for me. I remember walking home, sort of, but no matter how hard I tried, I just could not walk in a straight line. I stopped on the side of the road and put my hands on my knees. I was determined to get this walking thing under control. You *are* going to walk in a straight line, I told myself. But I couldn't. Somehow, someway, I made it home to my grandparents' house. They were still up, drinking and playing Yahtzee. I remember saying hello and then telling them I needed to go to bed. They were drunk and said their good nights.

I made it downstairs and made my way to the cot. An old army cot was my bed in the summer when I slept in the basement; it was cooler in the basement. I passed out, and the next thing I knew my dad was washing my face off, and I was on the bed upstairs. He had quit drinking during that period for about two weeks or so. "The old man quits drinking," he said as he wiped my face off with a cool wash cloth, "and the damned kid comes home drunk."

I managed a grin. "Just remember," I slurred, "you were a kid once." I don't remember how I got upstairs. He said he came home, found me in the basement, and smelled the booze on me. He shook me awake and took me outside and leaned me against the house, where I threw up. He carried me upstairs, took my clothes off, and washed the vomit off my face. It wasn't long before I was out again.

Then my eyes opened. What in the hell was that smell? There was a strong odor about the room as I woke up the next morning.

My dad walked in. "Not smelling too good in here is it?" he asked rhetorically. "Yup," he continued, "that's quite the smell there, kiddo." Good Lord, what was it? That's when I noticed that I had lost control over most of my bodily functions. Oh God, I thought, what am I going to do about this?

My dad walked closer to the bed. "I guess your friend had quite an accident last night; hit by a car." What in the hell is he talking about I thought. "I guess they don't know if he's going to make it or not."

Dear Tom,

I want to talk some more about that particularly tough time in your life. I know it's been on your mind. I'm talking about the time period roughly from 1979 through 1981.

There was a period when your wife filed for divorce, your mom died, and you lost your job. You lived alone until the lease expired, and then you moved back into your old room at Jack's house. That was tough as well. He was usually drunk and hostile, and he didn't want you there. What were you to do?

You believe that you simply didn't handle that whole mess very well. You believe that you didn't really have time to mourn the loss of your mom. You were too busy trying to hold your marriage together. You blamed your boss for incompetence when he fired you. But you really had it coming, didn't you? You drank during lunch hour. You showed up late to work. You just didn't do your job. You knew that. But you needed someone to hang your mistakes on.

You drank every day, and when drugs were available you took those. Anything to escape this life. You raided your mom's medicine cabinet and found some powerful pain medication. You took that as well.

Just a few days before she died, Jack asked you to take him to the gas station. On the way he talked about bringing your mom home from the hospital. He was drunk and rambling on about how much he loved her and could heal her with love. This was punctuated by occasional sobbing. You thought to yourself, "Leave me alone; don't lean on me. I have a marriage I'm worrying about. But you listened to Jack. You knew your mom was gone; she was not coming home, love or no love.

After you were separated, you picked up your daughter every Saturday. That was the highlight of your life. After you dropped her off, your heart would sink, depression would set in, and you would cry. Whenever you thought of your daughter you would cry. This happened frequently. You would be riding down the road when out of the blue you'd start crying. Drinking and drugging would make it all better.

You're not particularly proud of the way you handled the breakup of your marriage. The grass was always greener for you, but once you crossed the fence, you didn't want what you had found. It was too late. She had found someone willing to treat her well. Let's face it; you didn't. You weren't ready for marriage. There was partying to do. Having a fling with another woman was something to make you feel important, something you could brag to your buddies about. But it doesn't make for a good marriage.

So you asked for another chance, but emotionally she had moved on. You wished you had just let it go and moved on too. It took a long time for you to move on though. One of your greatest fears was the fear of being alone.

You didn't recognize the depths of your depression. You wonder sometime if there was something beyond depression. You were really out of it, and people noticed. You had an inkling of your alcoholism, but there was no way you were going to do anything about it. You were alone. Your mom was gone, your wife was an ex-wife, and you didn't have much of a relationship with your dad. It's an empty feeling being alone.

You didn't have any money, so you stole it from Jack to get by. In your mind you were worthless. It didn't get any worse. You were scraping the bottom. There were many times you went to bed at night hoping you would not wake up.

There came a time when you put it all behind you. You wanted to pretend it had never happened. You lived alone, and you drank alone; you had many empty relationships, but you had money, and you felt safe.

I think you need to forgive yourself. You had a disease. You drank and drugged. You were depressed, and you were not being treated. Hey, you fucked up; it happens. But you're taking steps to help yourself.

So today, forgive yourself, and let's leave it at that.

Later.

I was suddenly sitting up in bed. Oh, no, who was it? Had Mitch, Jake, and Ralphie made it home? It had to be Mitch. "Some kid by the name of Walter. I don't know, isn't he a friend of yours."

"No," I said relieved, "I don't know any Walter."

"Oh, I thought it might have been a buddy of yours." Resiliency made up for my lack of common sense; it must be hard-wired into most teenagers. I suppose that was the reason I was able to recover so quickly. Later that day I made it out to my mom and Jack's house. He had bought an old inn with twenty-two rooms. It was on a hill that overlooked a beautiful lake out in the country. The house was being remodeled.

My mother was thrilled. She could finally have all the material things she believed would bring her happiness. They didn't. I don't think they ever do. It was a cool and overcast day. I went down to the lake and thought about the night before. I had shit my pants! Good Lord, I had shit my pants! I was never, ever, going to drink that much again, I promised myself. But honesty was not one of my strong points. I broke that promise and many more over the next thirty years.

∽

Dear Tom,

Today is a bad day, a really bad day. You remember a dream. It happened many years ago. In the dream you were in the process of drowning. It was all right; you remember falling and looking up at the moonlight that was shining through the water. It was beautiful. You felt secure; nothing bad was going to happen.

As you walked by the pool today, you remembered that dream. You stared down at the pool, wondering what the water was like. Would it feel like silk on your skin? Would you want to wrap your arms around it? You thought maybe a couple of drinks might help you decide what to do. Today might be a good day to make that a reality.

Michigan, Late Summer, 1969

Maturity is a bitter disappointment for which no remedy exists, unless laughter can be said to remedy anything.

—Kurt Vonnegut (1922–), *Cat's Cradle*

CHAPTER 15

The dogs in the neighborhood started howling as soon as the fire whistle went off. It wasn't noon, so that could mean only that there was a fire someplace. The small, family-owned grocery store was on our way to The Shack, just across the street from the firehouse, so we stopped to pick up the usual assortment of pretzels, chewing gum, sweet tarts, and soda. We stepped outside just in time to see the fire truck rumble down the hill, kicking up dust. We stopped in our tracks.

"Where in the hell is the fire?" Ralphie asked.

"I don't know," I responded; but something in my gut told me that this was not good. All of us had a bad feeling about this. We exchanged glances.

We continued down the gravel road, and in the distance we saw the thick black smoke coming from the direction of The Shack. Then the fire truck stopped on the side of the road. My gut was right. It was The Shack, and there was no possibility of saving it, but for just a brief moment I thought they might. Our hearts sank. Not The Shack. Not The Shack. "Maybe it's not…." said Mitch, suspending reality for just a moment. But we all knew it was. So we stood there on the hill in silence and watched as The Shack burned to the ground.

CHAPTER 16

"So, Tommy, it sounds like you're really moving." "Yeah, I guess I am. You know, you guys should come out to the house. We could do some fishing, maybe have a few beers. There's a boat out there, you know." I was about to move in with my mom, Jack, my brothers, and some of Jack's kids. It would mean a different school. I didn't mind that much. I had my eye on the girl next door. My mom would tell me one day that I was "interested in anything with two legs." I wasn't sure what to make of the comment.

"Well, it's just bullshit that you won't be graduating with us," said Ralphie.

"Yeah, I know."

"Then why don't you stay here, man?" I had reached the end point with my dad. And living with my grandparents wasn't working either. At first my dad supported the idea, even encouraged it, but he held a grudge. When he was pissed he'd throw it at me by calling me "momma's boy." My brothers lived with my mom and it was just a better environment for a kid to be in—but not much better.

"I just can't stay here, I wish I could, but I can't."

My friends understood. "Yeah, I guess." Ralphie replied. We sat on a mound of beach sand just a short distance from where The Shack had once stood. It was a warm, late summer evening. I looked up and saw something streaking across the night sky.

"Hey, look at that," I said pointing skyward, "a satellite." Then all of us were looking at the stars.

"Where's the big dipper?" asked Jake. Now everyone was looking skyward.

"Let's see," I said. "It's right over there. See it?"

"Yeah, I see it." We stargazed for what seemed like a long time.

"You know what I want to be when I graduate?" I asked no one in particular.

"A bartender?" Mitch replied. We laughed.

"No, man, I want to be an astronaut or a pilot, something like that."

"I'm joining the army," said Mitch.

"You're nuts, man; come work with me at the station," said Ralphie.

"Nah. I'm joining the army. Vietnam will probably be over by then anyway." I turned to Jake. "What about you? What are you gonna do?"

Jake took a drag from his cigarette, "I have no clue, man; no clue." I believed then that my dream of becoming an astronaut was dead. Shoot, I was just trying to survive day to day. There was no alcohol that evening, which was a rarity for us. There was only security, friendship, good conversation—and that was enough for me. Today it was enough.

Florida, 2004

"No one can make you feel inferior without your consent."

—Eleanor Roosevelt

CHAPTER 17

"Tom, if you are not willing to talk about things, then I'm ethically bound to pursue other avenues for you. I have to recommend a treatment center. You've never been to treatment, so I think it would be a good idea for you to go."

I didn't want to discuss the past. I was tired of it. Jesus, we're talking over thirty year ago; time to move on. Okay, sure, my childhood sucked, but who didn't have a bad childhood. I really don't want to bitch and moan about my parents and my childhood that wasn't; I don't want to be a cliché.

"Treatment, what would that entail?" Treatment was nine weeks of outpatient care at a local rehab center for professionals.

The truth was that I had actually been to two treatment centers and hadn't succeeded in either. I had lasted a couple of hours in one and a couple of days in the other. Couldn't stand them; I felt like a caged animal. I needed to be in control, and in treatment centers I was clearly not in control.

"I'm going to leave," I told my rehab roommate.

"You'll be back," he said.

"Sure," I replied. "You take care of yourself."

"Here," he said handing me some AA books. "Take them. You'll need them one day."

On my way out I bumped into a counselor.

"You got a second?" he asked. "You know," he started, "usually, when someone here starts talking about leaving, we need to separate them from the rest. You know, they tend to take others with them." I nodded. "But you, I never had to worry about you."

"Uh, why is that?" I asked.

"Because you care more about them," he said pointing around the room, "than you do about yourself." He paused. "It was nice meeting you. Take care of yourself." He walked away and for just a second I thought of staying. He was right; I didn't care two-cents for myself. But I left, drove home, opened the refrigerator, and quickly drank a six-pack. I felt better. My dad was devastated; my brother wanted to kick my ass.

"All right, I'll try it; I'll try the outpatient thing." I had arthritis and stenosis in my cervical spine. The cause was never identified, but I thought it had something to do with stress. For years, I carried my shoulders up around my ears. Now I was in almost constant pain, and the only thing that relieved the pain was Vicodin. This time it was prescribed for me, and I was upfront with everyone about it. I didn't try to hide the fact that I was taking it; but I couldn't take it forever. Part of the reason behind treatment was to get off the Vicodin and on to something non-addictive. Evidently, there were other options; this according the physician on staff at the treatment center.

The antidote was a small, blue-green tablet that I placed under my tongue. It would relieve my pain and get me off this Vicodin habit. It worked in spades for the pain; I felt it kick in almost immediately, but by the time I had made the drive home, I was feeling ill, very ill, and I was as white as a sheet. I threw up continually, and I didn't feel well even the next morning. Apparently this was all part of withdrawal.

I called the center and told the story to the counselor who was assigned to me. "I can't take the medication I was given," I explained. "It made me violently ill."

"Tom, if the doctor here prescribed it, then I think you should continue to take it. He's a good doctor, and he has been dealing with these issues much longer than you have."

"What the fuck," I thought to myself. *"No,* the medication made me ill; I'm not going to take it." I didn't think this issue was up for discussion, but the counselor pressed on in a calm, matter-of-fact tone. "Well, the doctor here has years of experience with this issue, and he wouldn't prescribe it if he didn't think it would help, so I can't agree with your decision."

Now I was agitated. "You're manipulating me. I told you that the medication made me violently ill. Do you hear what I'm saying? Violently ill, and now you are telling me to take it?"

"That's my recommendation."

"Well, I'm not taking it. Good-bye." I later called and apologized for my outburst, but I never went back. I thought that I would not hear back from the therapist I had been seeing, but then one day he called and asked whether I wanted to schedule an appointment. Maybe we should talk.

∽

Dear Tom,

I understand you've been feeling kind of depressed, even a little anxious lately. You know, sometimes I worry about you. I know that sometimes life seems a bit hopeless. Sometimes out of seemingly nowhere comes resignation. For a micro-second you want it to be over.

I am writing because I think maybe it's time we talked about one of those touchy-feely subjects that, well, you know—that you don't like to talk about. I want to talk to you about your relationships with women. Yeah, I know. Makes you squirm a little. I tell you what. I'll write. You read.

You see, I was thinking the other day about your perceptions of girls when you were a kid, and about your perceptions of women now that you are an adult. I thought about some things that puzzled me. There's this paradox that I don't quite understand. Maybe you can help clear it up.

Here's the paradox: You like women. Hell, you love women. Always have. You enjoy their friendship. In fact you probably have had more female friends than male. But when these girls or women wanted more than friendship from you, there were times when you became, well, depressed, very depressed, and shameful even. These people only wanted sex, right?

That's how you felt. Am I on target here? Sometimes, as I recall, you'd literally run away from them, especially when you were a kid. You were bashful, clumsy, and awkward around girls. You hoped that maybe someday they might like you. They did, but they got too close, and too close is another matter.

Now I want to bring up something else that may be a bit embarrassing. I'm not a psychologist, but I'm bringing up these matters because I believe somehow they have an impact on your life today in ways that are not healthy.

Back to the embarrassing things I want to discuss. Don't get mad at me for bringing it up. Remember, you don't have to say anything. Just read.

A friend of my once said that some antidepressants put his "dick in the dirt." Now stay with me here. Isn't that what has happened with just about every women you've ever been with? Yeah, I know it's embarrassing. But maybe, just maybe, it's worth knowing why. What do you think? Eventually you overcame your problem. But why did it happen? I wonder.

Maybe you ought to just take a deep breath here. I recall your telling me of a dream you had. At least it seemed like a dream, right? One of those dreams that is so real that you can reach out and touch it, and one that you never forget. You know the one I'm talking about, don't you? The one where you're just a little boy of three, four, maybe five. Your mom was a stay-at-home mom when you were a young boy; most moms were in those days, and of course you were there.

In your dream she invited you into her bedroom where she was lying across the bed. She was on her stomach, and she did not have anything on below her waist. No pants, no skirt. You were between her legs. You were not entirely sure what to make of this. Was it a game? What were you supposed to do? Your mom said something, but you can't remember what it was. And what was up with the thermometer? Where did it come from? Why was it there? What was it for? You couldn't figure it out.

And where was your brother? Do you remember what you were feeling, what you were thinking? Do you think this has got anything to do with the fear you have of intimate relationships? Is it the reason you scratched yourself until you bled? Is it part of the reason you don't think you're worthy of the good life?

I wish I had the answers for you, Tom. I don't right now, but maybe together we can find them.

How does that sound?

And one more thing to think about. How can something like that be the fault of a little boy? It can't be. That I'm sure of.

Talk to you soon,

Your Friend

Florida, 2004

Anger makes you smaller, while forgiveness forces you to grow beyond what you were.

—Cherie Carter-Scott, *"If Love Is a Game, These Are the Rules"*

If you haven't forgiven yourself something, how can you forgive others?

—Dolores Huerta

CHAPTER 18

"I have some letters that I've written," I said, placing the folder next to me.

"Really? Who did you write them to?"

"Well, this is going to seem a little nuts; I wrote them to myself. I guess that's the only way I can talk about some of these things."

"Want to read them?" he asked.

"No," I said. "But I will." And I did. And there was something cathartic, something cleansing about writing and then reading those letters. Writing the letters uncovered memories of events that have shaped the way I live today. Some were beneficial; some were not. This was not about self-pity, although, to be sure, there is some of that. I don't walk around whining about my childhood or lack thereof. It was what it was; and it's brought me to the place where I am today.

My parents did the best they could with the tools they were given. Isn't that true for all of us? Resentment and blame moves us nowhere, and will ultimately only hurt the one holding the resentment. There is nothing gained by assigning fault. It's time to move forward. My mom passed away from cancer some twenty-three years ago. I remember the last time I saw her in the hospital. She couldn't talk; perhaps she didn't have the strength. I told her I loved her, and she gave me a knowing look. We both knew that it would be our last visit together—in this life anyway.

She waited for Jack to show, and, when he did, she passed away in his arms. My dad remarried and got sober. He is now a much different person, a better person. He's sorry about those days back in the late 60s and early 70s. He's told me that he regrets those drinking days and that he knows he was too rough on me. I prefer to think of the hours he spent playing catch with me and the time we spent in the backyard looking at stars—and those glorious sips of beer. We talk on occasion about AA and the problems drinking has created for both of us. I enjoy those talks.

As is typical, it was a beautiful morning. Something had changed on this particular day as I was driving along the bay. I noticed something very different about the way I was experiencing life. I was happy, content, and simply enjoying the day, living in the moment. I had always thought that going to meetings was enough work, and that somehow some magic would rub off on me. It didn't. I had to do the hard work. AA is an "inside job," they say, but it's worth the effort. No one wants to stay in the well forever; I'm making some progress, and I'm climbing out.

In 1972 I would move in with my mother and stepfather. I would see my friends on rare occasions; mostly on weekends, but over time I lost contact with them. Jake followed a job to Texas. He closed down the bar where he had been, and he was heading home with the last woman sitting at the bar. His car was estimated to have been traveling at over 100 mph when he missed the curve but not the tree. He was legally drunk—and then some. He died like he lived, with no feeling. Mitch dropped out of high school, ended up in rehab, and joined the Navy. He's happily married and has a son. He believes it's a miracle that he is alive today. He might be right. I hear he's taking each day, one at a time.

Ralphie has lived a troubled life. He was arrested for looking into the windows of bedrooms. He was also arrested for making obscene phone calls, and he was convicted of aggravated assault. The girl he assaulted was fifteen. When he's not in jail, he picks up odd jobs here and there. The gas station he thought he would inherit has closed down, and it is now just a vacant shell, overgrown with weeds. While he was a senior in high school he had a child out of wedlock. He doesn't see the child. Like father like son.

I think of my friends from thirty-some years ago. I think of the times we had at The Shack. A lot of good memories went with it the day it burned down. I look back at those days with an odd combination of fear and security—fear of living, but finding security in my friends. We found it in each other.

I went on to marry my high school girlfriend just a couple of years after graduating. We had a daughter, but we divorced four years later.

"How old were you when you married the first time?" a friend asked me.

"I was twenty," I said.

"Oh Christ," he said. "When you get married when your twenty, it doesn't count."

Maybe there's some truth to that. I think that I was still thirteen or fourteen emotionally. I still needed to grow up. After getting back on my feet emotionally and financially, I went back to school and earned a masters degree. After several failed relationships, and some seventeen years later, I married the kind of woman I thought I could never have. She has dark hair, brown eyes, and olive skin. She's drop-dead gorgeous. Along the way I learned that I'm not really that different after all.

We moved to Florida, a place I had always wanted to live. My wife and I are separated now; we have been for well over a year. Who knows what the future holds for us. I have two more girls, Catherine and Sarah. My first daughter Jennifer graduated from the University of Michigan, and she is the manager of a large retail store in a Detroit suburb. And, cliché or not, I do love them more than life itself.

On Father's Day in 2004, I called my dad to wish him well. As I was about to hang up I paused, "Say, Dad. There's something I want to tell you."

"Well sure," he said.

I paused again. "You did good, Dad; you did alright."

He paused, taking it in. "Well, you don't know what that means to me."

But I did. My dad is fallible like I am; like all of us are. But he's my dad and I love my dad. Today I'm no longer afraid of dreaming.

Dear Tom,

I was thinking about some of the better times you've had. Know what came to mind? Back in the summer of 1992, you rode your bike nearly every day. Sometimes during your lunch break at work you would take a quick 20-mile ride, go home, shower, and go back to work. Your favorite route took you along scenic Lakeshore Drive between Grand Haven and Holland, right long the coast of Lake Michigan.

There's nothing quite like a summer's day in Grand Haven Michigan. You lived in a small apartment that overlooked Grand Haven Beach and the channel. It was a perfect place for you. There was usually a nice breeze coming off the lake, and the waves sounded like a symphony. They rocked you to sleep at night. As with many other things, you became addicted to biking. You had all the right gear, and you had a beautiful Italian bike. Nobody, and I mean nobody, made bikes like the Italians. They weren't just bikes; they were works of art. This one was your pride and joy.

When you got on that bike, you were alive. You loved it. You had a dream of opening a bike shop one day. While the Michigan summers were to savor, the winters were not. How do you ride a bike in the winter? Well, the answer was a set of rollers that you set your bike on, balanced yourself, and simply peddled. You did that virtually every day in the winter so that by the time spring approached, you were ready to go.

You felt safe in that house, secure. It was one of the first things you checked out when you saw the apartment. It would work. You spent about seven or eight years in that little apartment. Oh, there were times when you were lonely and depressed. On several occasions while riding your bike on the rollers, you choked up and cried, not really understanding why.

You finished your ride, took a shower, and poured yourself a glass of wine—and all was all right again. Your drinking time was important to you. You didn't tolerate very well any interruptions to your drinking time.

Your life back then centered on your biking and your drinking. They seemed equally important.

On this particular summer's day, you headed down a road that ran parallel to Lake Michigan. Your legs felt good, as if they could just spin forever. It was a beautiful day with the sun on your face. You noticed the trees and how everything was green. Then something inexplicable happened. A grin appeared across your face. It seemed completely involuntary. It just happened. It was wonderful.

Life was good; it was real good. You wondered whether this was what it was like to be happy. You didn't know for sure, but maybe, just maybe, it was. That day you simply didn't care. That day you didn't care about money, relationships, or what you were going to do tomorrow. You had the sun, the blue sky, the trees, the green grass, the lake, and your Italian bike. And that was all that mattered that day.

You'd like more of those days.

They'll come, my friend. I promise.

Present Day

Acceptance of what has happened is the first step to overcoming the consequences of any misfortune.

—William James

Epilogue

Out of the whole of memory, there's one thing worthwhile; the great gift of calling back dreams.

—Antonio Machado

It seems as if this must be a Sunday in June or maybe in July. A light wind blows through the trees, and the sky is a deep blue. This is baseball weather. I notice the grass under my feet, and it feels cool and full. The radio is on with the sound of Nat King Cole's "Those Lazy-Hazy-Crazy Days of Summer." My dad is basting a chicken on the rotisserie; my mom is reading a good book under a shady tree. Our dog Spike is resting at her feet. My brothers are running back and forth through the sprinkler, laughing and having fun.

"Tom the bomb," my dad says, "how about little catch before we eat?"

"Sure. I'll get my glove." As I run toward the house to get my glove, my mom calls me over.

"Yeah, Mom, what is it?"

She reaches out and holds my face in her hands. "My boy," she says as she kisses me on the cheek. "My boy."

My brothers notice, and they want some affection too. "What about us, Mom?" my brothers say. They run over and get a hug and a kiss on the cheek.

I play catch with my dad. He shows me how to throw different pitches. "Turn your wrist like this," he says, "if you want to throw an inside curve, and like this for an outside curve."

My mom sets the picnic table, and my dad walks over to her, throws his arms around her, and tells her he loves her.

"I love you too, honey," she says.

- 117 -

*"Let's eat!" my dad says. There's conversation and laughter, lots of laughter.
"Tom," my dad says as we finish our meal, "it's supposed to be a good night to
watch the stars. What do you say?"*

"Sounds good, Dad. Sounds good."

Here I can dream.

About the Author

The author lives in Florida, and he has three inspirational daughters, Jennifer, Catherine, and Sarah. He continues his program of recovery, and he tries his level best to take it one day at a time.

978-0-595-35022-3
0-595-35022-4

Printed in the United States
127208LV00002B/283-285/A

9 780595 350223